Praise for *The Farther Shore*

"Short, sharp, devastating, *The Farther Shore* is a literary machine gun. Eck has written a winning debut that happens to be a war novel."
—John Mark Eberhart, *Kansas City Star*

"Bold, profane, hallucinatory. . . . Eck's spare, hard-knuckled prose proves well-suited to capturing the vagueries of American warriors engaged in nasty conflicts in forbidding corners of the globe."
—John Marshall, *Seattle Post-Intelligencer*

"Every horrifying aspect of war is captured in Matthew Eck's spare prose."
—Susan Salter Reynolds, *Los Angeles Times*

"Fear, banality, bravado, humor, pathos—it's all here, rendered in understated tones. It's astonishing that this is Eck's first novel."
—Michael Bonafield, *Minneapolis Star Tribune*

"Eck's writing is best when it vivifies the danger: making us feel the heat of the explosions, see the billowing black smoke or hear the sound of an antiaircraft gun 'burping its rounds off randomly.' Eck . . . bring[s] us straight into the devastation."
—Uzodinma Iweala, *New York Times Book Review*

"The first great war novel of our generation. The writing is often beautiful. And modern war has probably never been so fully explored as in this small, relentless novel. Eck never panders. We are not asked to cry, only to go quietly along for the ride."
—Stephen Elliot, *Salon.com*

"What Eck achieves in focusing attention on the identifying details of his setting is solidarity with post-Somalia soldiers, those who participate in post-September 11, 2001, conflicts and this new, post-modern style of warfare. The moral and logistical chaos of that experience—in all its terrifying specificity—is what will resonate. . . . Who could believe this of ourselves, he seems to say. And yet, here we are."

—Michelle Orange, *New York Sun*

"The first great 21ˢᵗ century war novel belongs to Matthew Eck, who captures the chaos and calamity of modern warfare in prose filled with characters who face a 'broiled darkness, where stunning violence, brutal death, dehydrated disorientation and an unnamed enemy are the least of their concerns when compared to the mental wreckage.' Support the troops—read this book."

—Todd Goldberg, *Las Vegas City Life*

"In concise language, this harrowing tale highlights the type of urban warfare now being waged: combatants are in the middle of not just one enemy but several warring factions, destroying the old rules of combat. In the end there is no sense of victory or even logic."

—Joshua Cohen, *Library Journal*

"A beautiful and shocking novel of war and youth."

—Heather Shaw, *ForeWord*

"As a war novel, *The Farther Shore* is a rich, distinctive page-turner. As a first novel it is exceptional, as well thought out as it is executed."

—Ryan Auer, *Bloomsbury Review*

"A haunting debut. Eck goes beyond the on-the-ground chaos of battle to capture the physical and psychological disorientation of modern war."

—*Publishers Weekly*

"Eck follows in Tim O'Brien's footsteps, emphasizing not the drama of the soldier's ordeal, but the painstaking, spirit-breaking, heart-wrenching details. A harrowing work that conveys chaos, confusion and raw fear."

—*Kirkus Reviews*

"Every word in Eck's first novel is as solid as stone. Every moment of crisis feels authentic in its terror and tragedy. Heir to Hemingway, and damn near as powerful as Cormac McCarthy in *The Road,* Eck has created a contemporary version of *The Red Badge of Courage* in this tale of one young man's trial by fire in the pandemonium of war in an age of high-tech weaponry and low-grade morality."

—Donna Seaman, *Booklist* (starred)

The
Farther Shore

MATTHEW ECK

MILKWEED EDITIONS

© 2007, Text by Matthew Eck
All rights reserved. Except for brief quotations in critical articles or reviews, no part of this book may be reproduced in any manner without prior written permission from the publisher: Milkweed Editions, 1011 Washington Avenue South, Suite 300, Minneapolis, Minnesota 55415.
(800) 520-6455
www.milkweed.org

Published 2008 by Milkweed Editions
Printed in Canada
Cover design by Christian Fuenfhausen
Cover photo courtesy the United States Department of Defense. Caption: "Explosive ordnance disposal (EOD) technicians survey the desert outside of Mogadishu for a safe site to destroy ordnance removed from a weapons cache during the multinational relief effort OPERATION RESTORE HOPE." Camera Operator: JO1 JOE GAWLOWICZ Date shot: 1 Jan 1993
Author photo by Katie Cramer Eck
Interior design by Ann Sudmeier
The text of this book is set in Dante MT.
08 09 10 11 12   5 4 3 2 1
First Paperback Edition

Please turn to the back of the book for a list of the sustaining funders of Milkweed Editions.

The Library of Congress has catalogued the cloth edition of this book as follows:

Eck, Matthew, 1974–
    The farther shore / Matthew Eck. — 1st ed.
        p.   cm.
    "Milkweed national fiction prize winner."
    ISBN-13: 978-1-57131-057-6 (acid-free paper)
        1. Mogadishu (Somalia)—Fiction.   2. Somalia—History—1991—Fiction.   I. Title.
PS3605.C55F37 2007
813'.6—dc22

                                                                                                    2007017509

This book is printed on acid-free, recycled (100% postconsumer waste) paper.

To

Katie

The Farther Shore

═══ ONE ═══

IT WAS FULL DARK, MIDNIGHT, AND HEAT LIKE THAT should have disappeared. Then the bombing started. Those poor souls, the poor fucks of the city, had no idea we were watching from the rooftop of the tallest building in town, six sets of eyes in the night, calling in rounds from the circling AC-130 Spectres. When they fired too close to the city's edge we'd make a call for them to move further out, into the unknown. When they veered too far out over the desert, and the city couldn't feel the shudders anymore, we made another call. It was a tightrope, a balancing act, a burden we adored. We were spotters on the roof, recon in a city controlled by warlords and their clans.

I was sick again from the heat. We'd been on the rooftop since before dawn, and now it was midnight and my eyes were tired from watching.

Fizer and Heath were in the stairwell, watching and listening for any sign that anyone threatening might be in the building. Flies shifted and settled on my hands and face throughout the night, trying to get inside my mouth, my nose, my eyes, and my ears.

There was a giant bunch of bananas painted on the side of the building that faced away from the ocean. On the ocean side was a banana tree with bunches of ripe yellow bananas. The paintings had faded under the hand of all that sand and sun. The building was empty of everything, looted and abandoned to the war.

Each of us was paired with a "battle buddy." It was Fizer and Heath, me and Cooper, and Santiago and Zeller. I was on my belly, watching the city to the east, and I could feel the heat left over from the daytime sun move up and through my body. The ocean existed out there beyond the city, some five miles away, but I couldn't see it through the darkness. The city itself was only discernable as a shadow, a little darker than the night sky. It was a long way down from the seventeenth floor, and other than the light of the stars there was nothing to illuminate the world below. I tucked my Night Vision Goggles back into their case. Using them gave me a headache.

Cooper was to my right, on his belly as well, looking through his binoculars out over the southern part of the city. He surveyed a large swath of the city, from the planes in the distance to the darkness in the street below. Zeller watched to the north. Lieutenant Santiago watched the west, but for the most part he strode back and forth among us. Perhaps he thought that's what leaders do, walk back and forth between positions, overseeing and sharing sympathy. He stayed low, crouched over so that anyone passing by below wouldn't see his silhouette if they happened to look up. But people never seemed to look up in this godforsaken city.

There were close to a million people out there, and most of them had probably just been scared out of their sleep. The city itself was maybe ten miles wide, but shacks and tents stretched far to the horizon outside it. There was no electricity, so it was completely dark at night. Most of the population was starving. In a briefing before the mission, we had been told that some two hundred people a day were lost to starvation, and that the dying were replaced by a steady stream of people straggling in from the countryside, searching for something better. The thought of all of those people, desperate and terrified, dreaming in the darkness, made me feel small.

Sand was everywhere, corroding everything. I rinsed my mouth out with water, but it was still there. It scratched at my flesh when I moved.

Santiago slapped me on the helmet as he passed behind me and said, "Stop thinking so much." Hunched over and chuckling, he walked away. He

repeated the line often. It was a mantra he was trying to instill in me.

A car turned down the street that led toward
my side of the building. One of its headlights was
out and the road was full of holes so that it winked
and bobbed before finally turning onto a side street.
Fighters wouldn't move around this way at night.
The danger in trying to see was also the danger of
being seen. All you had to do was aim at the headlights. No one with any knowledge, or history for
that matter, would want the enemy to see them.

There were two main clans in the city and they
had formed alliances based on tribes, family, friends,
and religion. One clan controlled the east, the other
the west. Each of the clans controlled villages in
the countryside when they wanted to, leaving the
city now and then to maraud. They made nearly all
their money on the black market, by stealing food
shipments, selling weapons, and by controlling the
borders and ports, and with them all of the country's exports. In our first month there, we'd come
to recognize individual members of the clans in
the villages. We would see the man with the wire-
rimmed glasses and the long scar on his cheek first
in one village and then a few weeks later in another. Somehow they'd find out where we were de-
livering food the next day. They'd move in on the
village, forcing out the locals. Then they'd collect
the food and sell it to the villagers after we left.

Outside one village we'd seen a dead body. It was impossible to determine whether the corpse was male or female through the cloak of bees and hornets that covered it. I'd never seen such a thing. As we moved among the villages, our Humvees kicked up so much dust that it never seemed to settle. Great flocks of birds shifted and turned as one on the wind, cutting down into the dust of our wake.

"Josh," Cooper said.

"Yeah," I answered.

"It's Sunday and I'm still afraid." He was trying to be as quiet as possible, so that his voice would disappear in the sound of the wind.

"Who's not," I said.

"Not too many people die on Sunday," he said. "Isn't that right?"

"True enough," I replied.

"No one wants to kill on Sunday," he said. Then we were quiet for a time, waiting on the bombing.

At one o'clock Santiago called over the squad radios for us to check in.

We responded in order of rank. As the only sergeant I was first, then Corporal Fizer, Specialist Heath, Specialist Cooper, and finally Private Zeller.

I crawled on my belly back to my rucksack and took out the binoculars, hoping to see the ocean again. As far as I knew I'd never seen the ocean before that day, and I'd never seen it at night. But when I turned on the night vision, there was nothing but the green glow of the sky and stars, and the dark shapes of the buildings below.

Before night fell, I had noticed that the rooftops were remarkably various, so that the city looked like a quilt spread out. If there was a cool wind blowing in off the ocean, I couldn't feel it here in the city.

Sitting on that rooftop, with all the heat and darkness, the city smelled like death. Enveloped by the stench, the thought of setting sail alone in this world horrified me. I shifted further back from the edge.

It was nearly two in the morning. The bombing would last until dawn.

I forced myself to peer out over the city again. Smart enough to be afraid, I kept my eyes on the darkness below. If anything shifted or turned I didn't want to be caught off guard. I couldn't make out the old van parked up the street, the one we'd used to sneak into the city. We'd rigged the stairwell in case someone tried to sneak up on us.

We'd been told that land mines were everywhere, hidden in potholes and crevices. Aside from the clans, there was no police force or local authority in the area. We had been sent in to restore some order to the capital and provide the people with some needed relief. The rest of the country had been subdued for the most part. This was the last, the worst of all the cities.

We hadn't come across any checkpoints on the way in, but we had been told that such stops were commonplace. There was always a fee to pay, and compliance was not optional.

Headquarters gave us the old van some twenty miles north of the capital. It took us more than two hours to drive the mostly unpaved road that connected the two cities, and then another two hours, staying off the main roads, to find the building we now occupied.

Cooper drove the van disguised as a civilian. He knew the language and some of the culture, and we relied on him to talk us through any checkpoints. We stayed hidden in the back, ready to attack anyone who discovered us. We had been told that most people supported one clan or another because they had to, and that their only real allegiances were to themselves and their family. But the clans were brutal and well armed. We were bombing the outskirts of the city in order to scare them into surrendering the territory they controlled without a fight.

My stomach turned and I felt dizzy. I was having a hard time holding even water down.

Santiago stepped up behind me. I closed my eyes and tried to relax for a moment. I felt as if the wind was being blown into me by way of a strange kiss, as if the city was breathing directly into me. The thick stench of shit and piss, along with the slightly sweet smell of death, smothered me like a blanket. Then I heard Santiago walk away from me and I opened my eyes.

I took a small sip of tepid water and spit on the ground next to me to rid myself of the sand in my mouth. The spit was dry and thick. I looked into the darkness below and at the door of the school across the street.

We'd arrived just before dawn that morning. During the day I watched what appeared to be a school across the street. There were children going in and out, along with a few adults. What was there to teach children in a place like this? How could they learn when armed gangs patrolled the streets and people strolled about with swollen bellies? How to focus when violence pervaded every moment?

We had more than enough water. We'd each brought two half-gallon canteens, along with three or four bottles bearing Arabic writing and rainbows. None of us knew where these bottles had come from. There was something mysterious about them, a touch of the exotic that made the water inside even more delicious, as if it had been drawn from some secret oasis.

"How are you doing?" Cooper asked, crawling to the corner between his side of the building and mine. He was both the medic and my battle buddy, so his interest in my health was twofold.

I moved toward the corner to meet him. "I'm here." Rocks scraped at my elbow and dug into my knees as I crawled over to him. Once there I brushed away the rocks that were pressed into my hands and looked at the indentions they'd left.

"Do you need another IV?" he asked.

"Not now," I said. Then I pulled a canteen from my LBE and took a small sip of water as a sign of goodwill, and because my mouth was dry. The water tasted like rank plastic. "I need some sleep."

"How long has it been?" he asked.

"Close to two weeks."

It was true. I'd been too scared, too nervous, too excited to sleep. I hadn't had a dream in the past two months and I was starting to worry that dreams had something to do with sanity and happiness. And I suspected that my sleeplessness had something to do with the way the world felt inside out, a thick, sticky mess.

"You can't die from lack of sleep," he said. "You just go until your body shuts down, forcing you to sleep."

"Sounds great," I said. I thought about it, the moment your body finally forced you to sleep, home at last.

"My stomach's still a mess," I said. I felt nauseous, as if I was upside down in the world and someone was trying to shake everything out of me.

"It's the sleep," Cooper said, "it'll hurt your stomach."

Soon the sun would be out, trying again to kill us. It was a hundred and twenty in the shade most days. I had shit on myself the day before and I was afraid the sickness might roll over me again without warning.

"If you fall out it's on me," Cooper said. "You should eat something."

"I know," I said.

"Even if you're sick it's better to try and eat," he said.

I'd been hearing this advice my whole life.

"You've got to keep your strength up," he said.

We hadn't been prepared for the heat. We were mainly a cold weather unit, the 10th Mountain Division, Light Infantry based out of Fort Drum, New York. And yet there we were in the desert.

People in other platoons were falling out left and right. They called out strange and often beautiful things as the heat finally forced them to race, face first, to the dirt and sand. Lopez, from first platoon, called out, "Where's the keys," before he fell victim to the sun. But no one carried keys into combat.

When I visited Lopez at the hospital, I asked him, "What the hell was that all about?"

"Hell if I know," he said.

But it had stuck with me nonetheless. "Where's the keys?"

The city shook under a heavy barrage of fire. Dogs howled all around us. Dust rattled into the air. The sun had baked the scent of death into the city's bricks, and it rose with the dust.

People gathered in distant streets, trying to see the sky over the desert. Our faces were camouflaged so they couldn't make us out if they looked up at the top of the building.

"Do you think Santiago's afraid?" Cooper asked.

"I think we all are," I said.

"This is fucking spooky," said Cooper.

"He knows what he's doing," I said.

Cooper looked up at the sky. "Still."

Santiago wasn't entirely stable, but I trusted him. I'd been on guard duty back at Fort Drum when the MPs brought him to stay in the barracks because his wife had filed assault charges against him. He was living too hard, but he often assured us that it was all a big lie, that his wife had been trying to get him in trouble for years.

And in any case, she was there with his two babies when we left by bus for Griffiths Air Force Base. He'd made some questionable decisions in training, but they nearly always seemed to be an effective way of dealing with the situation at hand.

They'd moved to the larger caliber guns, and the aircraft were concentrating their fire better. They were striving for a great opening night. They were desperate for the city's submission, desperate for perfection.

The Army was out there too, massing to the southwest and the northeast, along the main road that ran down the coast and through the city. We were to gauge the show of force against the level of resistance and report on whether the city was awed enough to accept help in forming some kind of government.

Santiago stepped up behind us, the radio in his hand. "Spectre Six-Two, Spectre Six-Two," he called. "Spectre Six-Two, Spectre Six-Two, adjust fire ten by ten north." He set the handset back on the receiver, then crouched behind me for a moment, watching my section of the city. He was careful to stay away from the edge, just far enough to avoid the view of anyone who might be looking up for a sign of us. I peeked over the edge briefly, but I didn't see a soul in the street below.

"How long do you think we'll be here?" Cooper asked Santiago.

"Don't ask me that," Santiago said. "Forever. Hell, I don't know. Maybe we'll leave you here. What's it matter to you anyway? What have you got to go home to?" He walked away before Cooper could respond.

"Just wondering," Cooper said. He was probably thinking about his virgin life and the girlfriend he planned to make his wife. The others gave him a hard time, saying that he had it all, that he had it all lined up the way a man should. It was such a lonely notion up there on the rooftop.

"We'll be home by Christmas, Coop," I said.

"That'll be good," he said.

"I heard it from Shane, at headquarters," I said.

"Can you imagine so many cities so close together that you wouldn't be able to see a single star for all the light?" He took his Kevlar helmet off and rolled over onto his back. "I've been there. Think about it," he added, as Santiago walked over. "One day you won't be able to see the stars because of all the light."

Santiago turned back to the bombing. Whenever a bomb exploded it briefly colored the darkness of the desert a bright orange.

"Bullshit," Santiago said. "You'd still be able to see them from the ocean." He knelt down and took his helmet off. He ran a hand through his cropped dark hair. "There's a lot of ocean in this world."

"If you got enough money to get out there," Cooper said. "People like us don't." Then he took a long breath, as if he were trying to smell the ocean through the city.

If I knew the names of all of the constellations and all those warriors, gods, and poets that they immortalized, I would have rattled them off, one after the other, for the amusement of Santiago and Cooper. But I know nothing about the stars.

Cooper and I relieved Heath and Fizer of guard duty in the building's only stairwell. It was three in the morning. Just two and a half more hours until dawn, and then we'd be at the stadium. There they'd pick us up in a Black Hawk and carry us out of the city, flying up the long stretch of coast, out over the desert they'd bombed, and back to the main camp a hundred miles to the north. Headquarters felt that getting out of the city would be the hardest part of the mission, so they were picking us up at the stadium, a massive structure no one had used for years. If for some reason they failed to pick us up there, we were to drive the van back out of the city.

The darkness in the stairwell was hard on the eyes. I was trying to see something where most likely there was nothing. Looking over the railing, down into seventeen floors of darkness, I tried to distinguish between the ground floor and all the nothing I was staring into. I wanted to believe that I could see the front door. Finally, I put on my Night Vision Goggles. The wide stairwell was such that you could see clear to the ground floor. They didn't make stairwells like that anymore.

I'd brought an MRE to try and get some nourishment. I set my weapon aside and tore the package open. It was a slice of ham. I could taste it before taking a bite. The smell of the juices and preservatives made me feel like throwing up. I put it aside and forced myself to eat the crackers, hoping that they would make me thirsty, and perhaps help me hold down some water.

We'd set up trip flares on the fifth floor and grenade simulators on the eighth and ninth, in case someone tried to sneak up on us. Santiago made us repeat this information aloud several times, so that we understood exactly where the traps were set. *Fifth floor flares* was a mouthful. *Eight and nine simulators* was easy to remember.

"Do you believe in ghosts?" Cooper asked, tearing the top off an MRE. I could smell aluminum and spaghetti. My stomach rose to my throat.

"I haven't decided yet," I said. "Why?" I was trying hard to listen to the darkness, but I knew that Cooper was trying to lighten the mood, so I let him talk.

He chewed slowly. The sound was nauseating. "I don't know," he finally said, "just that it's night. Don't you think violent places have more ghosts?"

"Maybe," I said. "Actually, I guess I don't really believe in ghosts. Maybe I haven't seen enough to convince me otherwise. We're always a little too eager to believe in just about anything."

"I just thought I'd ask," he said. "I'm scared. But I believe."

"Somehow ghosts seem less frightening here," I said.

"Yeah," he said distantly. "If that's what you think."

I could hardly make him out in the darkness. I couldn't even see my feet, so all I had to hold on to was his voice. "Cancer," I said, "now that's something to be scared of. Sitting in this building is something to be scared of. Meteorites, high school, the Muppets. That's the shit."

"Sure," he said.

"Wind chimes," I added.

"Wind chimes?"

"They freak me out," I said.

He let out a tiny laugh, probably just to let me know he heard.

"This girl, Angela," I said, "sent me a book when we were back at Fort Drum, about all the strange sexual things that have happened to historical figures. There was this guy, a poet I think, who was afraid of his wife's pubic hair. Think about that, the disappointment after the long wait."

"Yeah," he said. But he didn't laugh, and I wondered if he had even heard me.

"I can't wait to go to college," I said, hoping to bring him back.

"It's just this place," he said. "I never really knew it before."

"But you know more about it than the rest of us," I said. "You could go it alone if you had to."

Cooper had been born here. It must have been a strange place to return home to. Some are born to the war, and others are not.

"This is a bad place," he said.

"There are worse," I said.

"I know," he said. "I was just trying to be scared of something else."

"Fair enough," I replied.

Cooper had a heat rash on his neck, which made him look a little younger than he actually was. He was nineteen, with dark brown eyes, and he dreamed of going to college and getting a degree in architecture. When he laughed he was all teeth and slaps on the back. He would put his hand out to touch you, to let you in on the joke.

Cooper was the only virgin I knew. Or at least the only one that admitted as much. He was religious, more so than the rest of us, and I knew this had something to do with his virginity. Because we weren't the same religion, he'd already assured me that I wouldn't be at his wedding, that no outsiders would be allowed at his wedding. Otherwise, he said, you'd be the best man. It was a nice gesture. He had a girlfriend and he was waiting to marry her, waiting to be with her.

Cooper told stories about how he and his friends could get anywhere in New York by going underground. They knew every tunnel, every hidden passage, everything about underground New York. He'd promised to show me what he meant if I came to the city with him one weekend, but I never did. We were always making plans to go, but then something else would come up, something like going to Quebec for the weekend because someone told a story about the women and the bars. Or we'd go to Syracuse because we heard a rumor about a hot rod.

Cooper was the oldest in a family of eight. His grandmother had raised them after his mother and father were murdered just before he came to America. I never asked him about his trip across the water.

I listened to the night, waiting. When Cooper finally leaned back, the darkness and silence settled into the stairwell. There was a lull in the bombing. Even the dogs of the city were quiet. It was so still that I could hear the hum of my body. There's no such thing as silence, I thought, straining to hear something.

I stood and looked over the edge of the railing, struggling to see a few floors down in all that darkness. The stairwell curled out of sight like a tail. I felt as if the night was being pushed into me. I wondered how much more I could hold. Fear was in my eyes and in my ears. The buzz of mosquitoes filled the air. I slapped at them a few times, then gave up.

I let Cooper fall asleep, and got to wondering what people out there in the city were dreaming about. Then I wondered whether any of the girls I knew back home were dreaming about me at that moment. I was eager to fall in love. I'm always falling in love. Leave me alone for a moment and I'm falling in love with the very idea of a woman. But we always love what is lost to us, so all I could imagine were girls I'd never see again.

Leaning against the railing, I stood and looked down into the stairwell. I couldn't see anything, but I listened intently to the night.

At first I thought it was the wind, but then I could distinguish voices. Someone was whispering at the bottom of the stairs, and somehow I knew that they were going to make their way up to us. They were careful to be quiet, but I heard steps, like the soft tap of the tongue against the roof of the mouth. They sounded far away, yet their silence was more threatening than anything that could be spoken.

I touched Cooper lightly on the shoulder. I didn't have to say anything. He was quickly awake and aware enough to not make a sound. He stood and stepped to the door that led onto the roof, opening it just enough to let a tiny sliver of light appear on the floor. Then he let it close gently. I keyed my squad radio so that the others would know something was wrong.

Suddenly the stairwell filled with the silver light of a trip flare. Cooper quickly opened the door and motioned the others in. Santiago pointed for Cooper to stay where he was, and then he started down the stairs two steps at a time, the rest of us falling in behind him.

We stopped on the ninth floor, waiting. I pointed out the trip line for a grenade simulator on the floor. Then the other grenade simulator went off on the eighth floor and something red and burning hot shot up through the stairwell and past my face. It looked like a piece of metal.

Santiago pointed for Heath and Fizer to stay where they were and then the rest of us continued down the steps, two or three at a time. We could make out their shapes by now, two of them, running. I saw the shape of a gun in the darkness and dove to my left down a hallway. They were retreating down the stairs. Using the wall as cover, I found a target but held my fire. I followed it for a moment.

Then there was a blast from the stairwell behind Santiago and me. Zeller lit into the darkness, his weapon rattling to life. My ears filled with a tremendous ringing. I started down the steps after Santiago. He cleared the distance between himself and the figures quickly, firing heavily into them.

It was nothing but the red light of tracers by now, because I couldn't hear. Rounds ricocheted off walls and I worried I'd get hit by one of the bullets. Then the firing stopped for a moment, until Zeller fired a three-round burst that dropped one of the targets. The figure went down and Santiago pointed Zeller to the person's aid while we moved on, hunting the other one.

As we moved past the fallen figure I told myself not to look, to keep going. If you looked at the fallen you paused long enough to join them. I followed Santiago, clearing with him to the next floor. I took aim at the target myself, but then noticed Santiago out of the corner of my eye, tracing the running figure. He took a knee and aimed. It was a difficult shot, but he dropped it.

We moved toward the person he'd shot, and then Santiago waved me past, pointing for me to clear all the way to the bottom of the stairs, in case there were more. My ears were still ringing, and I couldn't hear a thing. There was still a long way to the bottom, and I didn't want to separate myself from the others just yet. I walked down a few flights, then stopped and put on my goggles. There was nothing. I looked up the stairwell and saw Heath and Fizer moving toward me.

"What the fuck happened?" yelled Heath. He was close to me, screaming in my ear. He was dripping with sweat, and I could smell him.

"I don't know," I yelled back.

"What do we do?" screamed Fizer. The two of them looked at me, waiting.

"Hold the front door," I said, pointing them down the stairs.

"We got to get out of here," Heath muttered.

"Hold the door," I said.

Heath shook his head and the two of them started off again down the steps.

I found Santiago and told him we needed to move. Then I looked down at the body. It was small for a man. Santiago bent over the figure with an unrolled compound press, the loose white ends dangling beside him. He stood and said something, but at first I couldn't hear over the ringing in my ears. Then he was screaming and it came to me in slices, getting louder, then duller, until I finally got it: "They're just kids."

"I saw a gun," I said.

"It's a stick," Santiago said, pointing at a stick on the floor.

"This one's dead," Cooper said over the radio.

Santiago called Cooper down because the one he'd shot was still alive. The boy didn't make a sound, but he was obviously fighting for his life.

"You and Zeller get the gear," Santiago said, pointing toward the roof.

Running up the stairs, I slipped in the mess that Zeller had made of the other child. I stood slowly and walked carefully. I told Zeller we were to grab everything.

They were all standing in a circle around the wounded boy when Zeller and I returned with the gear. The ringing had subsided enough that I could hear the others breathing heavily.

"Goddamn it," Santiago said to Heath and Fizer, "you two should have stayed at the front door. I'm not about to lose my squad because you two can't fucking listen." He pointed them back down the stairs.

The boy had a hole in his chest. Cooper applied pressure to the wound.

"We got to go, Cooper," Santiago finally said, grabbing him by the shoulder and lifting him to his feet. The pool of blood beneath the boy was expanding steadily.

Then we were down the stairs and out in the street. Standing in the open air, it was as if we'd set off a chain reaction. Machine guns echoed in the night, answering to the shots we'd fired. People seemed to be firing at the sky, down alleys, and all around us. It was as if we'd given a signal.

The van was gone.

"I can't believe this," Santiago said.

People standing in doorways turned their heads to watch as we jogged up the street. My rucksack dug into my hips and shoulders and my M-16 clicked like an insect as the shoulder strap bounced lightly against the weapon. My socks were already soaked in sweat. It was ten miles to the stadium in the southern part of the city.

Most of the people we passed didn't really seem to care about us. They were just like the inhabitants of any big city when something disastrous strikes: some were eager to stand on the porch and watch their neighbors suspiciously while others were curious to see what might happen next. But in this city, where people were routinely hacked up with machetes, shot in the streets, or dying of famine and disease, they'd seen it all before.

Men with Kalashnikovs passed us indifferently, moving in the opposite direction. We might as well have been ghosts to them, haunting the wrong time and place.

When we heard vehicles approaching we hid in doorways or ducked into alleys in case they were the technicals we'd heard about, old trucks mounted with machine guns and rocket launchers. At one point we hid in the front yard of what looked to have been a great mansion. We stood among empty pots and planters, in an area where a beautiful garden once thrived.

About halfway to the stadium we stopped near a fountain that was the only decoration I could see in a massive plaza. It had been about forty minutes since we left the building. Kids mulled about. The fountain was empty and we took a seat on its lip. It was still unbearably hot in the city, but somehow the wind gave me a chill.

An astonishing number of children milled about in the plaza. This was a city for desolate and abandoned children.

Mangy dogs roamed among the children, in groups of three or four. For the most part people ignored them, but if they got too close people kicked them in the ribs.

There were vendors everywhere. Heath walked over to one of them and bought a beer. Santiago watched him.

"You brought money?" I asked Heath when he joined us again.

"You didn't?" he replied.

"I couldn't think of a reason," I said.

Santiago took a five-dollar bill out of the little cover in which he carried his ID card. He walked over and bought six beers from a man as if he were simply a tourist. When he came back he handed one to each of us. I knew my stomach couldn't handle it, so I put mine in my rucksack. The others sipped at theirs.

I watched the kids walking around us. They looked us over closely, inspecting our faces, uniforms, patches, and weapons.

When Santiago finished his beer he rolled the empty bottle toward a massive statue of a horse in the center of the fountain. The horse was the color of sand. Rearing back on its hind legs, it appeared to bite at the sky with its open mouth and menacing face.

As we were leaving the plaza, we hid in a doorway as an old truck rattled past. It was ludicrous, a junker of a truck mounted with a giant Russian anti-aircraft gun. A pickup truck followed, with about fifteen people packed in the back and hanging from its sides. They were armed to the teeth, and appeared to be prodding the city for something.

It took us several hours to jog from the plaza to the stadium. Once we'd arrived, we hid inside. Everyone breathed heavily as we sat in seats about halfway up from the field. The city roared dully behind us.

"Are you sure no one followed us?" I asked Santiago. He'd been at the rear of the squad.

"Give me the radio," he said.

He tried the radio, but it didn't make a sound. He switched out the battery for a new one. Still nothing.

"Is it broke?" asked Zeller. He already knew the answer. We all knew the answer.

"You mean we only have our squad radios," I said.

We sat back in our seats. I put my feet up on the back in front of me, and dried my face briefly with a T-shirt from my rucksack. I took a sip of warm water and rinsed my mouth before spitting it out. I took another small sip and swallowed.

Next to me, Cooper emptied his canteen with loud gulps. He breathed heavily, and when he exhaled sweat and spit fell onto his shirt and pants.

Santiago took his Kevlar off and lit a cigarette. I wanted to remind him that a burning cigarette could be seen from miles away. It was a lesson Santiago himself had taught us before we left, illustrating it one night in an open field. "I am the light of this world," he'd screamed at us from across a field, a cigarette held out in front of him to make the point. "This little light of mine," he sang, "I'm gonna let it shine." Everyone was stupid in Santiago's world.

"When they can't get us on the radio," I said, "they'll come looking. They know to find us here." It was true, this was our extraction point.

"It's just that it would have been nice to let them know that we started something," Santiago said.

"We smoked the fuck out of those kids," Cooper said, staring at the field.

"Yeah," I said. He said *smoke* as if meaning to invoke the spirit world, as if it were an offering.

"Yeah," I said, "we smoked the fuck out of some kids." It made it sound like a light show, a matter of smoke and mirrors. Almost as if it could be undone.

"I was born here," Cooper said out of nowhere.

Two dead boys. I tried to picture their faces, but I couldn't. It was the same with love, I'd once been told. When you are away from the person you love, a girl once told me, if you can't see their face, that means it is love.

The bombing seemed to be subsiding. I wondered whether the grand strategy would really work. Maybe you really could scare a city into submission. We'll just wait here, I thought, and they'll come for us soon enough. The night was giving way to daylight, to a full-fledged Sunday morning.

My ears hummed and my head felt heavy. I leaned forward and rested my head in my hands. So this was what combat is like, to engage the enemy and fire your weapon. I felt renewed in the world, alive and well. The heat of my sickness was gone, replaced by a sensation of light and power. I leaned further forward, smiling.

═══ TWO ═══

THE CITY PACED PAST DAWN LIKE A WATCHFUL DOG, never returning to sleep. The bombing had stopped hours ago. We'd made our last radio check somewhere just after midnight, and now we were all wondering whether the Army would ever miss us.

"They should be here by now," Fizer said.

As the sky filled with soft light we moved up toward the press box. Climbing the concrete steps, I had the sense that this day would be different, and I tried to understand what I had learned the night before. I felt as if I had been tempered somehow, as if I would now see everything differently.

The door to the press box was gone and the room had been gutted. The windows were smashed and broken glass crunched beneath our boots. Sections of the window frame hung loose in the opening, and pieces of glass jutted out here and there. Looking out over the field and the stands, I felt like a man at the controls of a machine that had broken down. I remembered hearing in a briefing that they'd once held the Goodwill Games here. Whether it was true or not, the notion held me for a moment, the gathering of nations, the attempt at peace and camaraderie. All the flags displayed, crisp and colorful in the wind.

The track and the soccer field below were in miserable condition. Football, I thought, they must have called it football. But then between the warlords, the desert, and an approaching army, the groundskeeper didn't have the most desirable job. It was probably hard enough to get grass to grow in this place. The field had no shade, and so the grass had been burnt away. The dirt was yellow. I imagined the UN staging a match for the city, Italy versus Germany, or America versus some much smaller country. They'd pass the ball around and between us. They'd kill us in all that open space.

"Where are they?" Heath asked, dropping his rucksack to the floor. He let out a loud sigh as he settled down to sit on it. He scratched at the red stubble that had grown since we arrived in the city.

I thought about the boys, dead in the hallway. Someone would have found them by now. They were no longer among the missing.

"Maybe they're waiting for more light," Fizer said, turning to Santiago for confirmation.

Santiago nodded. "Probably. They know we're here. They know where to find us."

Except for Santiago, we all dropped our rucksacks on the floor and used them as seats to avoid the glass. Santiago leaned over, looking out the broken window. Against the backdrop of sky and the shattered window, he looked too weak to be leading us. He looked altogether ordinary, not like a leader who inspired confidence. He finally put his rucksack on the floor. His back was wet with sweat and white patches of salt stained his uniform.

"Jesus Christ," Cooper whispered, a prayer forming on his lips, as if he'd just grasped what really happened in that building. Softly he whispered, rocking back and forth with his hands folded together and his head bowed.

I turned to look out the window again, but Santiago was watching me. There was something frightening in his eyes. It was the recognition of something that he wasn't about to share with the rest of us.

After looking at me for a long time, he said, "What do you think?"

"Sit here for a while," I said. "We shouldn't move around much during the day." I looked at the floor and the broken glass. "You sure no one followed us?"

"We'll take our time," he replied, "but we do need to figure something out. Just in case they haven't dispatched any helicopters for us, or in case something happened to them."

"Why wouldn't they dispatch the helicopters?" I asked. "They haven't heard from us in hours, and they know this is the extraction point if anything goes wrong."

No one was talking or even looking at anyone else. I wondered if they were thinking that there was no way to go it alone if the Army didn't come for us. Or maybe they were thinking that the only way to get out alive was to go it alone.

I sat in the corner, leaning forward on my M-16. The hand guards were cool against my cheek. A morning breeze blew into the booth, and I felt myself drifting off. For a few minutes each day, just as dawn broke, the earth cooled briefly before giving itself back over to the desperate heat.

Santiago called for an ammunition and food check. Each of us still had at least seven full magazines of M-16 ammunition. Fizer had four belts of SAW ammo. Cooper, Santiago, Zeller, and I each had two MREs left. Heath had one, but Fizer didn't have any because he'd eaten all three of his on the rooftop.

"Think the clans are looking for us?" Cooper asked.

"Two dead kids," Santiago replied, "they'll be looking for somebody."

"We left enough trash and brass behind that they'll figure it out," I said. "They'll know we're U.S. Army."

Santiago looked at me, "You don't think we got all the trash?"

"No way to be sure," I said. "I guess we could dig through our stuff and get a rough idea." I was thinking about the MRE I'd been eating in the stairwell. I had no idea what happened to it. Our safety and our good names, not to mention the integrity of the entire mission, could hinge on the importance of a few bits of trash.

"I'm not worried about the casings," he said. "That could be anybody. But if we left any trash behind we're in a world of hurt."

"Why?" Fizer asked.

"Our intentions were good," said Cooper.

"Maybe they won't figure it out," added Heath. "Maybe they won't even find the kids, maybe they were just reacting to the gunfire."

"They'll find them," I said. "They always do." Nobody cared much for this remark. They all turned away from me and looked vacantly out the empty windows.

I wondered if the parents of the dead children could possibly forgive us. But I knew better. If you killed children, I thought, the world stirred in the end, and somewhere someone would be expecting justice. No one said it, but the real question looming over us was whether the city would discover us before the Army.

Just as an awkward silence settled over us, I heard a UH-60 Black Hawk rotor beating faintly in the distance. I'd been in the cavalry long enough to distinguish the sounds of different helicopters. The UH-60 was heaven or hell, life or death, depending on who you were. We held our breath, but it turned and flew off in another direction. The slap and thump followed in its wake, a retreating wave.

Then there was another one, a lone Cobra. They were gathering, several of them now, circling and moving toward us. We all stood, and we could just make them out as small dots on the horizon. Santiago told us to put our rucksacks on and to get ready to run down the steps to the field below. The helicopters were cutting in fast, flying low over the rooftops. It was gorgeous, beautiful, exactly what we'd been longing for.

My rucksack was heavy, and it bounced around on my back and hips as I ran down the steps. We stopped at the bottom and crouched behind the low concrete wall that separated the field from the stands.

Just as the first UH-60 began to descend into the stadium, an RPG sailed past it unexpectedly.

The helicopter pulled up clumsily. Another Black Hawk tried to land and we started onto the field to meet it. But as it settled in the middle of the field, another RPG sailed out of one of the long tunnels that led onto it. We watched as the mouth of the tunnel slowly filled with a motley assortment of fighters. Then the .50 caliber and the minigun on the UH-60 started firing into the tunnel, and we all made a break for the helicopter.

The enemy was fast and there were enough of them to cover the ground between us and the helicopter. Cooper was running a few feet in front of me when he took a bullet and doubled over to the ground. I grabbed his LBE strap and dragged him back to the low concrete wall where Santiago and Zeller had retreated. The stadium was filling with smoke. They had us pinned down.

Cooper was bleeding profusely from a wound in his chest. The helicopters weren't doing much good. Bullets hit the wall in front of us and cracked overhead. Cooper's lips quivered, but I couldn't tell whether he was trying to say something or simply to breathe. I put my head close to his lips, but I couldn't hear a thing. I pushed a compound press down over the wound. I'd never touched another man's blood before. I tried to imagine that it was something else.

"We've got to get to that bird," yelled Santiago.

"We won't make it across with him," I said. "They'll tear us up." But I knew that we had to move.

Santiago lifted Cooper into a fireman's carry and we all took off for the helicopter, bullets flying around us. We didn't get far before an RPG sailed close overhead and we hit the dirt, Santiago falling awkwardly beneath the weight of Cooper.

Then another RPG flashed past the tail of the Black Hawk and into the stands behind us. The explosion seemed small and weak for a moment, then it was deafening and the world went silent. After a few confusing moments I could hear again, barely, through a high-pitched whistle in my ears.

As if to join the small amount of smoke emanating from the stands, a puff of black exhaust kicked out of the engine of the UH-60, which seemed to shudder as it pulled back up above the field, the door gunner firing at the tunnel. I saw Heath and Fizer in the helicopter next to the door gunner, firing their weapons as well.

The helicopter shook and sputtered. There was a hole in the tail of the aircraft, and more dark smoke coughed out of the engine. Then suddenly a large caliber gun opened up at the helicopters from another tunnel. It looked to be mounted on a light truck.

"I can't carry him alone," Santiago said. There was blood on his cheek and shoulder.

Zeller grabbed Cooper's legs and the two of them carried him toward a tunnel.

A Cobra helicopter set its nose at the truck and fired. A rocket crashed into the truck and that part of the stadium sagged with the weight of the explosion. Now rockets were flying from all directions. I could feel the dull chop of the blades as the helicopters turned and tried to land again. The air was thick with black smoke that tasted like burning metal.

Then suddenly the helicopters turned away. I felt the thud of the rotors as they faded into the distance. They were leaving us there.

After a brief pause, Santiago pointed toward a large opening across the field that looked like the main gate. Santiago and Zeller each grabbed one of Cooper's LBE straps, I slung my weapon and grabbed his legs, and we made our way toward it. We went unnoticed through the smoke and stench of the wounded.

As I ran, I gagged and spit to get the taste out of my mouth. We moved forward, surrounded by moans and unintelligible curses. Beyond the smoke, the world was all eyes. I tripped over a body and braced for a scream, but there was no response.

As we made our way out of the stadium, I took a single look back and saw a woman trying to emerge from the smoke. She was dragging herself along the ground, wounded badly. I thought for an instant of shooting her out of pity. I remembered something I'd heard once: Never leave the dying alone long enough to remember what they'll become.

But then I felt the tug of Cooper's weight as Santiago and Zeller resumed our rush toward the sunlight.

═══ THREE ═══

WE CARRIED COOPER FOR ABOUT AN HOUR BEFORE WE were overcome by exhaustion. We moved south from the stadium, through a maze of alleys, dead ends, and cul-de-sacs, which made it impossible to keep a pace count or to use landmarks for direction.

We stumbled into the first hotel we came across, but the old man working the counter explained with hand gestures that it wasn't actually a hotel. The doors all had numbers on them, and several were half-opened and full of watchful eyes, but the man insisted that it wasn't a hotel. In any case, we would never understand him entirely without a conscious Cooper.

Then a woman who appeared to be the man's wife appeared, and the two of them began to argue about something incomprehensible. We looked over at a young man who appeared to work there loung- ing in the corner. He stared out at us from a set of mirrored sunglasses, wearing a smile pitted with the pink of gums and the dark of a few missing teeth.

"Not a hotel," Santiago said to no one in particular. "Fair enough." There was hate in his voice, real malice, and he was a horrible man when he lost his temper. The world was quickly slipping away from us. We nodded at the man and his wife and moved off in another direction.

The sun was rising and with it the heat. There were people on the streets, nodding at us indifferently as we passed.

We carried Cooper awkwardly. He stared up at the sky and mumbled vaguely every now and then. The sky was a lush blue, almost unbearable, and the scattered clouds were full and thick. Cooper was getting heavier by the minute, as if everything that was draining out of him was being replaced by something weightier.

At the next hotel we pounded loudly on the door, shouting out for the owner. When he appeared it was obvious that we had woke him, although it was a little late and too hot for sleep. At first he looked at us as if we were figments of his imagination, or perhaps scraps of his dreams that could be shouted back into the street or some receptacle of sleep. Armed and wearing our desert BDUs with the American flags sewn on the right shoulder, we must have made quite a picture. But when he spoke it was in excellent English.

He said cheerfully that he'd gone to Berkeley. Then his mood seemed to darken. He wanted to know how we'd pay. We gently set Cooper on the floor.

"Is he okay?" the owner asked.

"He'll be fine," I said. "Do you have a phone?"

He shook his head. "Not for years."

"Just watch the door," Santiago said.

I trained my M-16 on the front door, irritated by his tone.

Santiago leaned on the counter and stared at the man. The man smiled back without blinking. The whites of his eyes were yellow, his cheeks fat like a child's.

Still watching the door, I took a knee on the floor next to Cooper's body. I told him in a low whisper how his girl and his mother would never forgive him if he died. I told him how he'd made it out before and that he'd make it out again.

"A room," Santiago said to the owner. "We need a room now."

The man nodded. "All American?" he asked.

"Hell yeah," Santiago said. He looked tired, horrible and defeated. "You will be reimbursed by the Army."

The man looked us over. He was looking for something he could use, some way to gain an advantage.

"Cash," the man said.

Santiago looked at me and Zeller. We both shook our heads.

"We have dog tags and identification cards," Santiago said. "I'll be glad to give you either one to hold for reimbursement."

"I don't know about that," I said.

Santiago raised his hand to shut me up.

It didn't seem like a good idea to me, giving someone all the information they would need to find you in this world: name, rank, and social security number. They'd even know your height, weight, and the color of your eyes. That would surely be enough to follow you home and find you.

"I need cash," the man said. "Everyone knows about you by now. I'm taking a risk by even talking to you."

"What do you mean everyone knows about us?" asked Santiago.

"Word travels fast," he replied.

"If you tell anyone we're here I'll kill you," Santiago said. "I don't care anymore. I'll shoot you in the fucking head."

"I don't care enough to tell anyone," the man said. "People kill each other here all the time."

Santiago stepped around behind Zeller and opened his rucksack. He took out Zeller's Walkman and a few cassettes to go with it.

"Gift?" the man asked, stretching his hands out eagerly.

"Gift," said Santiago.

"What kind of music is this?" the man asked.

"All kinds," Santiago said. He looked down at the tapes. "Country."

"Country," the man said, as if he was trying to remember whether he'd ever heard that kind of music before. "I always like jazz. The Beatles. Chicago. We have music here, but it's hard to find. And it's too expensive."

We asked for a room on the top floor and he gave us a key. He didn't tell us where to go before he disappeared into a back room, smiling down at the Walkman.

The numbers on the doors appeared to have been torn off or stolen. Zeller and I carried Cooper, trailing along behind Santiago as he tried the key in one lock after another. We'd walk a few steps with his heavy body, let him gently down to the floor, then pick him back up and move a few more steps.

People spoke in hushed voices behind the doors, and often just after we had tried a key in their lock the door would open and someone would look out to see who had passed. Children ran down the hallway, darting between us as we searched for our room.

One of the doors was wide open, and sure enough, when Santiago tried the key in the lock it was ours. I was relieved. Nobody died in hotels, I told myself.

Before we put Cooper on the bed I tied another compound press over the one that was already saturated with blood. Then I gently set my gear down in a corner of the room and began to look around.

I found a young girl in the closet. Her shirt barely covered her belly, and she was wearing nothing more than a dirty pair of underwear with a piece of rope tied at the waist to hold them up. She was climbing all over me in no time. She smelled like piss and onions.

"Can you get rabies from these things?" Zeller asked, poking a child away from the door.

All the children were laughing and pointing at me.

"They like you, Stantz," said Santiago.

Suddenly they were barking at me like dogs. Apparently I was destined to be a leader of dogs in this country. Then they started another game, holding hands and dancing wildly.

We quickly shooed out all the children except the first little girl. She wouldn't let go of my arm. I asked her to warn me if anyone with a gun approached the room, but she didn't understand a word. Then I told her to scream if she saw someone with a gun, acting it out by pointing my weapon and letting out a little yell. She practiced screaming for me between laughs. "That's nice," I told her, but there was no use. She obviously didn't understand. Finally, she ran off looking for the other children.

We left the door to the room open. Zeller sat in the doorway on guard duty. Children strolled up and down the hall, peeking into our room as they passed.

Just off the main room was a tiny room with a pipe in the floor and shit on the walls. It smelled like the end of the world, so we closed the door on it.

I could hear afternoon prayers echoing in the street. I'd heard them the day before from the rooftop, but now they seemed louder and more threatening. I couldn't remember the last time I'd said a prayer.

We decided to open the windows to let some air in for Cooper, but when I tried them they were all stuck.

"Jesus Christ," Zeller said, pushing me angrily out of the way. He struggled with the first window, but then it shook loose and opened. The other ones were no easier.

The compound press on Cooper's chest was black with blood and dirt. He had a satisfied look on his face, as if someone he loved was whispering to him. The corners of his mouth turned up in a faint smile, and his face was darkened by a thin beard and heat rash. I thought about holding his hand, but instead I just let it hang off the edge of the mattress, palm up and open. I should have folded them across his chest.

Santiago stepped up next to him, poured some water on an extra T-shirt, and pressed it to Cooper's forehead. His eyes were open and shot with blood. Santiago asked Cooper to drink, but he didn't respond. Then Santiago started asking him about New York City, in the kind of voice people use with young children. Finally he took his hand and felt for a pulse.

Blood seeped slowly from under the edges of the compound press, collecting dirt and sweat as it moved down his arm to gather in his palm. I was reminded of the dams my brother and I used to build in our dirt driveway. We'd turn the hose on at one end of the drive and build stream beds and dams to contain the flood. The water balled up with the dirt, and the balls of mud looked like mercury. But in this case Cooper's blood was seeping slowly into the mattress.

Santiago paced the room while I sat in a corner on my rucksack. We took our helmets off. The band in mine was stained dark brown from all the sweat. As the day grew hotter the sounds of the street gave way to nearly total silence, as if the city were empty.

"What do we do now?" Zeller asked, stepping in from the hallway.

Santiago shook his head. "We wait for dark."

"We should find help," I said. "There have to be doctors in this city. Maybe we could ask the owner."

"Too many people already know where we are," Santiago said. "We don't know who's who in this city. If we go to the wrong person it's over for all of us." Then he stopped pacing and put his hand on the wall opposite me, next to the window.

We had a corner room so there was plenty of city to see. Directly across from the hotel was another building that looked to be abandoned. Then there were just small houses lining a road yellow with dust.

"We need to keep moving," I said. "He's not going to make it much longer."

"We fucking stay here until we figure something out," Santiago said. "No shit we got to move, but how?" He was leaning against the wall, his M-16 slung across his back. "You tell me, what do we do?"

"We steal a car," I said. "It doesn't matter, we have to move. We can't wait for them to come back for us."

"I know," Santiago said quietly. "Trust me, I know. They're definitely looking for us. But we need to rest so we can move out later. Clear our heads."

He looked over at Zeller. "I don't think Cooper can take the move anyway."

Zeller turned to us from the door. "Do you know where we are?"

"No," Santiago said. He looked at me. "You?"

"I couldn't keep track," I said. "This place is fucked." I took out a map of the city and spread it on the floor. "I think we're south of the stadium."

Santiago took a knee next to me and we looked at the map, retracing the path we took to the stadium and then trying to recreate our path from there to the hotel. The city looked so small on the map.

"It's what, fifteen minutes east to west by car," I said. "We could be back at the place where we picked up the van tonight."

"Yeah," Santiago said. "But they're probably setting up roadblocks as we speak. They've probably blocked all the routes into and out of the city. We can't move right now." He looked at Cooper again. "We can't even speak the language."

Still watching from the door, Zeller asked, "How long will they wait there?"

"Two days," Santiago said. "Maybe more." He stood back up and resumed pacing the room.

I stood to stretch and to gather myself. All the windows were open, but still, it was absolutely stifling in the room. I found the rules of engagement printed on a notecard inside my Kevlar. I wanted to read them again, to see what it said about shooting children.

I'd heard of gangrene. I'd heard you could follow the path of an infection from the wound to the heart by looking at the veins, which turned a dark, horror-movie purple. I thought I could smell the wound as well, though it was hard to tell over the stench of the city. Poor Cooper just wasn't responding.

"I don't know," I said, "it doesn't look good."

Santiago was looking at Cooper's fingers. They were swollen and purple.

The room was unbearably hot. I longed for a breeze, to smell the ocean in the distance. The wind was coming in from the desert, but it brought no relief. There were dozens of flies in the room as well, and they weren't shy. Dogs barked endlessly in the distance.

I looked at my compass briefly, then stood and walked to a window to see if I could make out the ocean. There was nothing but city as far as I could see, and it all looked to be covered by a film of yellow dirt. I went back to my corner.

Santiago tried the radio again, but to no avail. He pulled the batteries out and looked them over. They were brand new. He put them back in and clubbed the radio on its side.

"Sometimes that works," he said, hitting it again. He stood and lifted the radio above his head for a moment, but then lowered it to the floor next to his gear.

The bolt in my M-16 was filthy with sand. I broke the weapon down and took out my cleaning kit. I thought of how the weapon had locked up, just when I needed it most. "I'm going to go ask the owner about a car," Santiago said. "We've got to get out of the city. It'll get worse before it gets better, and I don't think Cooper can wait. You two stay here."

When Santiago left, Zeller spoke up. "Where will we go?"

"Anywhere but here," I said.

"At least he listens to you," he replied.

"Sometimes," I said.

"Do you believe him?" he asked.

"Believe what?"

"That we need to wait. Cooper's going to die if we don't move."

"Santiago's right," I said.

Zeller let it go. "How far away do you think the Army is right now, or at least those who are looking for us?"

"I don't know, a couple hours," I said. "I haven't heard any helicopters."

I went back to my weapon, looking up every now and then at Zeller. He was staring at the ceiling.

I wondered if he had a better chance of making it alone in the city because he was black. I was white, Santiago was Hispanic, and Cooper was dying.

I finished cleaning my M-16 and put a light coat of oil on the bolt and assembly before closing it up. When I locked it back together, I made sure the safety was on before chambering a round.

Zeller was still staring at the ceiling. I wondered if he was as tired as me. "You can sleep for a while," I said. "I'll watch the door."

"Too tired to sleep," he said. Zeller was from Tupelo, Mississippi. He'd been recruited to play football at a number of schools in the south, but Zeller had the misfortune of being from a family that valued military service over college. Serving in the military was an obligation in his family. In fact, he needed an honorable discharge from the Army in order to stay in his grandfather's will.

Zeller was almost as tall as Santiago, and he probably weighed about as much, but unlike Santiago, Zeller hated work. And he loved smoking cigarettes. When we were still at Fort Drum in New York, I would often hear him wake up in the middle of the night, and I'd turn to see him sit straight up in bed, light a cigarette and smoke it, his eyes still closed in sleep.

Santiago had been gone for more than half an hour when I started to worry. I hadn't heard anything suspicious or troubling, which led me to think that maybe he'd left us behind. It would be dark soon. Sunday night.

"I heard they hate us here," Zeller said. "Black Americans."

"Why?" I asked.

"I don't know," he said. "That's what James at HQ told me." He took out a cigarette and lit it. "I kind of wanted to ask one of them when I got the chance."

"Well, this is your chance," I said.

He smiled and tossed me a cigarette.

"Probably just a rumor," I said. "Besides, what does James know?" He was quiet for a long time, and then I said, "Do you think they'd like me?"

Zeller smiled. "The motherland," he said. "That's what Coop said when we left for this place. He said Africa's the motherland and we're going back home." He stared at his boots and picked at one of the laces. "Motherfucker."

I looked over at Cooper. Things weren't turning out the way he'd expected.

The young boys' faces flashed back into my mind. We'd killed two children, the Army hadn't been able to extract us, and now we were surrounded by city and sin, with no real plan for the chase ahead.

And here was Zeller, trying to figure out who he was and how he fit in this place. "You heard him talking about it, didn't you?" he asked. "You heard him talking about the motherland?"

"Sure," I said. "It's all he talked about." Actually, I had never heard Cooper talk about the motherland. I just knew that Zeller wanted to talk, and that he wanted me to listen. And when he was finished, I wanted to share a story about Cooper that I remembered Cooper telling, about a time he went to a cave as a young child. They were deep in the cave when the lights went off and the tour was left in total darkness. Cooper said he wasn't afraid. Then when the lights went back on the guide told them that they wouldn't see any spots. Total darkness did that, Cooper said. He'd told me the story one night when we were on guard duty. The whole time he was telling it, he never stopped looking up at the stars.

Cooper was dead by the time Santiago returned. Zeller and I hadn't even noticed when he died. He'd been too far gone by the time we checked into the hotel, but still.

Santiago spread a T-shirt over Cooper's face. Cooper and his laugh, I thought. The way he had to touch someone when he laughed, as if he were letting them in on a secret.

I closed my eyes and tried to cleanse my mind of any image of this room. I didn't want to remember it. I never wanted to be there again.

≡ FOUR ≡

WE SAT THERE QUIETLY FOR SOME TIME, LOST IN OUR own heads. As the light gradually faded on the ceiling, and the day gave way to dusk outside, the only sound in the room was Santiago's footsteps as he paced. Finally, he spoke.

"Okay, so the owner doesn't have a car. He did say that there are buses and trucks that give people rides for a fee. He also said that he would give us enough money to ride out of the city for something in exchange. We can try and find the Army out there."

He turned and looked at me, perhaps waiting for a sign of agreement. "They don't run on Sundays though, and they don't run at night, so we have to wait until tomorrow. Besides, he says we have a better chance if we try it on Monday. By then he could sell some stuff and get us more money for bribes."

He shook his head in disgust. "He says the clans have set up more checkpoints, which means we'd probably get caught on a bus. He also says it's hard to steal cars here, because people will do anything to protect them. But if we give him some stuff he can sell he'll give us some money in return, and then we can try to buy a car or bribe our way out." He started looking through his rucksack. "We've got to have something for him."

When he was finished with his rucksack he looked at me and then down at my gear. He walked over. "What do you have?"

"I only have a few books in here," I said. "They're not worth much, but you can take them." I handed them to Santiago.

He stood above me holding the books, weighing them in his hands. Then he went over to Cooper's bag and placed my books on the floor next to it. "I guess we could take something out of his bag," he muttered.

"He wouldn't mind," I said.

Santiago kicked Cooper's rucksack with his foot, almost as if there were something hiding inside that he had to scare out. "I'm really sorry, Coop." He stood facing away from me, lost in thought, and then turned slightly and asked me over his shoulder, "Do you know what he has in here?"

"Same as everyone else," I said. "Walkman, maybe a magazine. I think he has a watch."

Santiago looked in the front pocket first and found Cooper's watch. He seemed relieved to have found it right away. It was a normal Army watch, with hands that glow in the dark. "This should work," he said. Then he found some tapes. "Jesus Christ, look at this shit." He laughed a little. "How could anyone listen to this crap?"

It was true. Cooper had horrible taste in music. He'd spent too much time with his grandmother. I'd often told him how important it was to know what kind of music to use in order to set the mood. He'd tried to listen to music that I copied for him to use with his girl, but he never could get into it. He liked the stuff his grandmother sent him: show tunes no one had ever heard of, bad movie soundtracks, and the new song of salvation for the week.

I looked out the window and watched the last light fade in the sky. Then, as my vision shifted down to the building across the street, I saw a man waving at me. I quickly ducked away from the window. "There's someone over there. He waved at me." I peeked back across and he was still waving.

"What?" Santiago asked.

"There's a white guy in the building across the street." I looked again, and the man was still waving. "He's fucking waving at me."

"Bullshit," Santiago said. He crept to the window and peeked out himself. He quickly drew back into the dark room. "I guess you better wave back."

When I looked out the window and waved, the man gave me a thumbs-up sign.

"He just gave me the thumbs-up," I said.

"Probably Special Ops," said Santiago.

The man motioned for me to come across. "I think he wants to talk," I said.

"Guess you're our man," said Santiago.

"I'm not going over there," I said.

"I'll cover you from the street," he said.

I followed Santiago down to the lobby and out into the courtyard. The few sparse trees looked larger than what I remembered. Santiago stopped in the doorway and we both looked out at the street.

"You'll be fine," he said, his hand on my shoulder.

"I know," I said, without much conviction.

I stood there for a long time. There was no wind, no sound, nothing but the silence of the night. My legs were uneasy, my head felt empty, my stomach hot like it was full of liquor.

Santiago smiled and put a hand on my shoulder. "Don't worry."

My mouth was full of saliva, like right before you throw up. I spit. Waited. Then I spit again.

"He's one of ours," Santiago said, and pushed me toward the door.

I peered up the street in either direction. I couldn't see far, but there was no sign of movement. I ran across the street, my 9mm bouncing in its holster.

I struggled to keep my head clear and my nerves steady.

When I reached the other side of the street, the man was standing in the dark just inside the doorway, an Army-issue Colt .45 in his right hand. He nodded and smiled as I walked through the door and into a cavernous room. He stepped to the door behind me and looked up the street in both directions.

"What's your name?" he asked.

My back was wet with sweat. I rubbed at my neck with my hand and felt the grit of sand. "Cooper," I said. He had no reason to know that my real name was Joshua Stantz. I couldn't see his face, so I told him I was Cooper.

"You the ones from 10th Mountain?" he asked.

"Yeah," I said.

"Hamlin," he said. "You can call me Hamlin for now."

"You here to help us?" I asked.

"Come on up," he said, and started toward a stairwell. He had a southern accent. I'd heard it when I was in basic training back in South Carolina. He walked slowly in front of me, which made me feel more secure.

He stopped at the foot of the stairs and pointed a few steps up. "Watch out," he said, "fishing line." He turned when he spoke, and I could see the silhouette of his face against the darkness of the stairs. "The sound of someone falling is more than enough to wake a man up. Loud noises ruin your judgment and instinct." He stepped over the fishing line. "Understand?"

"Check," I said with false confidence, bending over to touch the fishing line. It seemed like something a real warrior would understand entirely. Santiago loved that kind of information.

"That's good to know," I said. I wanted to impress Hamlin. I wanted him to like me, and I wanted his help.

"Do you know the language?" I asked.

"Probably," he said.

We walked into the room he'd set up directly across the street from ours. There were several windows, and he stood between me and one of them. He was short and stocky, and as my eyes adjusted to the dark I could see that his black hair was streaked with the yellow sand of the streets and desert. Sweat parted the dust on his face and made swaths of shiny skin. He was wearing a pair of dirty old khakis and a short-sleeve cotton shirt, much like most of the men in this city. A .50 caliber sniper rifle and an AK-47 were lying on the floor.

I wondered if he was one of those men the government didn't acknowledge or recognize if they went missing. We'd heard rumors. A man like him didn't exist to anyone. He didn't have any Rules of Engagement to follow. He made the rules.

"Do you have any extra food with you?" he asked.

"We're almost out," I said. "We can barely take care of ourselves."

"Ruin travels fast," he said.

I didn't know what to say, so I nodded in response. He waited, expecting me to say something.

"It's hard," I said finally.

He nodded in agreement and motioned for me to sit on a small wooden crate in the middle of the room. I wondered what the building had been used for originally. Other than the crate, all that remained in this room was an old wooden desk that was missing all its drawers. It had been flipped on its side, and now Hamlin was leaning on it.

"Do you have a radio?" I asked.

"No," he said. "It would only compromise my identity if I were killed."

"Why'd you call me over?" I asked. "Are you here to help?"

"Do you realize that I could have shot you if I wanted to? I could have killed everyone in that room and no one ever would have known."

"Yeah," I said. "I'm sure you could have."

"I'm just fucking with you," he said. "There was no reason for me to shoot you."

We sat in the middle of the room, away from the windows. I looked at the ceiling in an effort to avoid his stare. Even in the dark it was unmistakable.

"Your friend is dead, right?" he asked.

"Yeah," I replied.

"He must have been hit by that big anti-aircraft gun," he said. "Something heavier than an AK-47."

"I know," I said, not wanting to appear as if I didn't know the truth, or didn't get the joke. The room lightened a little with the rising moon. The way he was looking at me made me afraid to move. I ran a hand through my hair and felt the sweat and the sand.

"Kids," he said, staring at me. "I mean, they have twelve-year-olds doing the fighting for them. They're just kids."

I tried to see in the darkness. I wondered whether there might be another door or even another room that I couldn't see.

He walked to the window and looked across the street toward our room. "You've had a hard time of it," he said. He put his Colt .45 on the inside window ledge and picked up his sniper rifle. Then he pointed it up the street and moved his head gently until he was looking directly through the scope. Someone was walking up the street. I could hear the sound of footsteps on the stone.

"You just can't catch a break," he said quietly.

"There's no luck to be had in this place." He followed the target down the street, moving the weapon delicately with every step it took. "It's ruin and the rhythm of ruin," he whispered. "You just can't escape it in a place like this." He gripped the trigger firmly and almost seemed to stop breathing.

"Where are you from?" he said, leading the target. There was no air in his voice, and I wondered how he produced it.

"New York City," I said, continuing as if I were Cooper.

He let out a small grunt.

But the question prompted me to think for a moment of my parents' home back in Wichita—of their back patio and red picnic table. I would have liked to tell him about the passing storms, dark and radiant over the plains. The way they made the horizon look long and full of light, as if you could pass through all that space and distance unharmed.

"You're young," he said. "What brought you here?"

Accidents and intentions, I wanted to say. That's what a friend of mine from Missoula always said about why he joined the Army. That was the kind of thing a friend would point out to you, and that was the way a friend would phrase it, so you would know that something kind was being shared.

But I couldn't remember what had brought

Cooper there to die, so after a moment's reflection I said, "College money."

He looked at me disdainfully for a moment, and then turned back to the scope on his rifle. A cloud swept across the moon and the room darkened momentarily.

His look reminded me of what happened during my graduation ceremony on the last day of basic training. We were standing in long ranks on the parade field when the division sergeant major walked past inspecting us. Unexpectedly, he stopped in front of me and asked, "Why did you join the Army?" I gave the same answer I had just given here. He shook his head and moved through the rest of the ranks. When we were dismissed, my drill sergeant pulled me aside and took me behind the bleachers while all but a few other soldiers, alone like myself, went to be with their families and friends. He made me do push-ups and sit-ups until I puked.

"Do you think you're better than me?" my drill sergeant asked.

"No," I told him.

"Good," my drill sergeant replied. And then he said that he didn't even graduate from high school, but he'd bet money he could fuck a woman better than me. I couldn't even do two hundred sit-ups without getting sick, he yelled. How could I ever expect to satisfy a woman? He left me there to ponder his question with puke on my lips and shirtfront.

Hamlin and I were quiet for a long time. He looked up the street, still following the target. I watched the back of his head. It looked soft in the darkness.

I wanted to get back to Zeller and Santiago. The memory of that exchange with the drill sergeant made me uncomfortable, not least because he was actually a kind man, and I genuinely respected him. We're all afraid of something, and sometimes we go about things the wrong way.

"Are you following us?" I asked.

"I'm here for someone else," he said, "for one of the warlords. They want to make a point, to scare the fuck out of all of them."

He stood the rifle against the wall and walked back to the crate. Then he took a pocketknife out of his khakis and started digging under his thumbnail. "Do you have a safety pin?"

"No," I replied.

"Not even across the street?" he asked. "What about the others?"

"I'll ask," I said.

"Look," he said. "I just wanted to tell you to get out while you can. That's why I called you over here. The Army's not coming back for you."

"What?" I said. It was too dark by now, and our room across the street wasn't visible from where

I sat. Santiago would be watching from the court-yard. He'd be getting impatient for my return.

"They won't be back in the city anytime soon," he said. "They lost a helicopter trying to get you out."

"They'll be back," I said, "that's why we're here. They're moving into the city soon."

"Things have changed," he said. "They're no longer massing outside the city. They're pulling back to the port cities north and south of here to wait out the rain."

"Rain?" I asked.

"It's going to rain soon, heavy rain, and you boys don't have what it takes to live through it."

I wasn't afraid of rain. "Why should we be afraid of the rain?"

"A monsoon," he said. "Same time every year."

"But they're starving," I said. "Why can't they grow anything if it rains every year?"

He shrugged his shoulders.

"Come on," I said, "you must be able to help us."

He shook his head. "I'm here for someone else." A fly landed near the corner of his mouth and he brushed it away. "It's none of my business," he said, "but between us, did you shoot those kids?"

"No," I said. A vehicle was moving up the street.

"That's good for you," he said. "You should be

all right." He picked up his rifle and followed the vehicle along the street.

"What should we do then?" I asked. "What do they want us to do?"

"I don't know," he said. "I didn't ask. Didn't expect to run across you out here. If I were you, I'd do my best to get out of town. You can't make it here. These people will murder you for nothing."

When I couldn't hear the car anymore he turned to me and said, "You should go now, it's dark."

I walked down the stairs slowly, mindful of the fishing line. As I left the building and crossed the street I imagined him leading me, moving the sight forward slightly with every step I took. I could sense the weapon trained on my head, the weight of the trigger against his finger.

"What took so long?" Santiago asked. He seemed agitated.

"He wanted to talk," I said. We turned and began to walk back to the room.

"I thought I saw him following us," Santiago said.

"The fuck you did," I said.

"I said I saw him."

"Check," I said, but I knew that he was full of shit. That he hadn't seen anyone behind us. That you never knew who was following you.

Once back in our room, I didn't waste time. "He said we need to leave before it starts raining."

"Before it starts raining?" Santiago said. "What the hell does that mean?"

I told them what Hamlin had said about the Army retreating to the ports north and south of the city. Then I told them about the monsoon and how we couldn't make it here alone.

"What do we do with Cooper?" Zeller asked.

"What do you want us to do?" asked Santiago. He sounded angry, as if this conversation had already begun to play itself out while I was gone.

"What do you think we should do," Santiago asked, "take turns carrying him on our back?"

"He goes with us," Zeller insisted.

"We're in deep shit here, and you want to go dragging a body around?" Santiago was angry. "He'll be just fine if we leave him here. We'll come back with the Army later."

"Maybe we can find some other clothes," Zeller continued, as if he hadn't heard Santiago. "We can pretend we're reporters or something. Like we lost one of our own in the city."

"And what'll we do with our weapons?" Santiago asked.

"I don't know," replied Zeller. "Leave them here with Cooper."

"We're leaving Cooper here," Santiago said. "You

get into a whole different set of rules of engagement when you take on a disguise."

"So long as we get out alive, what does it matter
what we wear?" I asked.

Santiago shook his head, then walked to the
doorway and looked down the hall. Zeller walked
over and sat on the bed next to Cooper. He was far
braver than me.

"I thought we were never supposed to leave
anyone behind," Zeller said, his head in his hands.

"Someone else will come back to get him," said
Santiago. "When the Army finally gets here. We'll
arrange things so that no one else can have the
room, and then we'll come back with the others."

"Look—," said Zeller.

"We fucking leave him here," Santiago said, turning to Zeller. "We'll get him later, okay?"

Zeller rocked back and forth on the mattress,
but in the end he nodded in agreement.

"We leave him here," Santiago repeated, quietly
this time.

Santiago sat in the doorway watching the hall. It
was just before midnight. Time moved slowly in
that room.

"What if we say he shot the kids?" Zeller asked.

I felt as if things were getting away from us.

"What do you mean?" Santiago asked.

"I mean Cooper shot those kids," Zeller said. "You know they're going to look into this. And they're going to have our asses if they find out. I mean, we all killed those kids."

"I didn't fire a shot," I said, "but this is crazy. Let's just worry about getting out of here."

"What the fuck does it matter if you fired a shot?" Zeller said. "You were right there with us."

"It was an accident," Santiago said. "And what about Heath and Fizer? They've probably already talked about it."

"We'll say they got it wrong," Zeller said. "The two of them weren't even with us when the kids got shot. Did you say anything about it to them? I know I didn't. We didn't say shit to each other in that stadium, and they didn't ask. They fuck people for mistakes like this. They fuck you for life, man."

"They'll look into it," Santiago said. "Once you start lying it gets messy."

"They don't hang you for honest mistakes," I said.

"How do you know?" Zeller asked. "You're in this just as deep as we are."

I could tell by the way Santiago walked to the window and looked out that Zeller had at least planted the idea. Santiago shook his head, and as I watched him it suddenly occurred to me that I couldn't stand him. In fact, I didn't have much respect for any of my superiors.

"I'm still in charge here," Santiago said.

"We need to fix this," said Zeller. "We need to get our story straight."

"There is no story," I said. "Just two dead boys and Cooper."

"We'll figure this out later," Santiago said. "We go it alone, tomorrow night, no matter what."

They were past listening, and I didn't say anything else. I didn't want any part of their mistakes and stories. It seemed to me as if Santiago was merely trying to keep control, while Zeller was concerned about protecting himself.

All I wanted at that moment was to search out the center of my soul, to find that tiny point that kept my body alive and my memory from storming. Sundays always seemed to be the saddest days.

We took turns pulling guard duty, but no one really slept. The hallway seemed longer in the night, but there was no movement. My eyes ached from the effort to see beyond the darkness, to find spots of light in which I might see the enemy.

When Santiago came to relieve me, he asked how I was doing.

"I'm here," I said. "Which is something."

"It's something all right," he said.

I took one last look down the hall before standing up to make room for him. He put his M-16 on the floor next to the doorway, then looked at me and smiled.

"Jesus," he said, "I'm going to fucking kill myself after this one."

"Why?" I asked.

"Why not?" he asked with a chuckle.

"Fair enough," I said.

"Which is to say you don't care," he said.

"I didn't say that," I said. It was far too late for a joke.

"We'll be fine," he said. He put his fist out toward me and I touched it with mine. "Just get some sleep."

Back in my corner, all I could do was stare at Cooper. I couldn't turn away from him. Each time I closed my eyes I imagined him springing to life. After some time I forced myself to stop, and my thoughts turned to times when I hadn't done enough to save others as they went down into the swell and disappeared beneath the waves of this world. And there I was standing on the farther shore, hoping they would surface again.

Then I opened my eyes and Santiago and Zeller were there. But poor Cooper truly was somewhere else.

═══ FIVE ═══

ON MONDAY MORNING I SUDDENLY WOKE UP TO FIND Zeller on top of me, kneeling on my arms, hitting me in the face and neck. I struggled, but I couldn't shake him. Finally, Santiago dragged him off me. My face felt like it was on fire. I was sure that my nose, my cheeks, and my eyes were all broken. I rolled toward Cooper for protection, not knowing what I'd done to bring this on.

"What the fuck is wrong with you?" Santiago shouted at Zeller. But Zeller didn't know. He couldn't remember what had happened. He said I'd been tearing at the waking world again in my sleep, writhing around like a madman. Before he knew what he was doing, he was trying to kill me. The sight of me sickened him, he said.

"Fucking asshole," I said to him. My head hummed like a hive of bees.

"Fuck you," he said.

"I'll tell them you shot those kids," I said, angry.

Zeller lunged for me, but Santiago had him by the neck. "Don't touch him," he said. He shoved Zeller hard into the wall. Zeller tried to break free, but Santiago had him in a hold, and he couldn't breathe. Santiago held him there, letting him suffer.

There was a weak knock on the wall beside the doorway. The owner asked us from the hall, "Maybe you kill yourselves in there?"

Santiago trained his M-16 on the man as he walked in and looked around the room. A trail of Cooper's blood ran from the doorway to the mattress, and there was a mess of gear on the floor. Santiago checked the hall, then took a seat in the doorway so he could watch the room and the hall at the same time. The owner sat on the bed next to Cooper, his back to Cooper's body. I heard the dull roar of a plane high overhead.

"All it takes is for one of these people to go tell one of the warlords that you're here," the owner said. He looked at me as he spoke. "You don't look so good," he added.

"I haven't been sleeping well," I said.

"Very interesting," he replied. Then he told us that his American name was Michael and that he'd wanted to be a banker. That he'd wanted to make some money.

"Who doesn't?" said Santiago.

He told us he liked Americans. He'd try to help

us. He promised us water and a little food. "But things are so difficult and expensive here." He looked around the room at our gear. "A weapon might be worth something. Or maybe a watch or a Walkman. You need to leave. The monsoon rains are coming." He leaned forward onto his knees. "Soon it'll rain for a month. The roads will close and the desert will turn to mud."

"So we've heard," said Santiago.

The Army had never said it would rain. Not in one of our briefings. They had talked about fire and famine. They said this place represented the future of the world unless we took steps to stop it. The briefings themselves came to serve as their oracle.

"You need to leave tonight," Michael said. "Once the word gets out, you're worth nothing more than the reward."

"We're leaving soon," I said.

"How much are they offering for us?" asked Santiago.

"Enough," Michael said.

"We'll leave after the sun goes down," said Santiago.

"Just remember," Michael added, "they'll kill you if they find you. Everyone knows by now that you killed those boys. And once they know you didn't make it out of the city they'll hunt for you."

He stood up and stretched, then lingered, waiting for a payment. "The warlords buried those boys in their cemetery, where they bury no one but themselves and their own families."

He walked to the window and looked down at the street below. I wondered about the sniper across the street, but I didn't say a thing.

"This used to be a nice city," Michael said, "and I'm sure it will be again. But now everyone is a criminal. People are robbed of their houses and their families, their children and their wives." He fell silent for a moment. "And then there's the rape." He turned from the window and looked down at Cooper, then up at Santiago. "And you think you can make it better?"

"Why haven't you turned us in?" asked Santiago.

"Why would I?"

"Because you like Americans," I said.

"I really don't care who is ruining this place," he said, "I just don't like to see people die."

"Can you help us find a car, or at least a ride out of the city?" Santiago asked.

"That is impossible," Michael replied. "You will have to take a truck or a bus like the rest of us. I'll help you find some food and water, and money for bribes." Then he walked over and looked down at my books. Santiago had left them on the floor next to Cooper's stuff.

"You can have them," I said.

"They're not worth much," he said.

"They're dead weight to me at this point," I said. "Take them."

He nodded. "Thank you."

Santiago walked up behind him. He reached into Cooper's bag and took out his 9mm. He pushed the release and the magazine fell out. Then he dislodged the chambered round and checked to make sure the weapon was clear. He handed it to Michael.

Michael held it by the barrel as if it were nothing more than a stick. He stared at the weapon, sizing it up. It looked like something he'd done before. In cities like this one, you paid with whatever you had. And sometimes you paid with whatever could be taken away.

"I'll see what I can do for you," Michael said, and turned to walk out of the room.

We'd been in the city for two days now. I went through Cooper's bag and found an MRE and a canteen full of water. It was our last meal, and the last of what Cooper had for us.

When I picked up the canteen to take a drink it felt like bad luck in my hand. I poured a little water into my cupped hand and looked at it. But I couldn't stand the thought of drinking his water. It was as if something of him was still in it. I turned my hand over and let the water fall to the floor.

I suddenly realized that Santiago had been watching the entire gesture. I turned to look at him and he stared back at me. Then he looked down at the tiny puddle briefly and turned back to the hall.

The MRE was a slice of ham with au gratin potatoes, crackers, peanut butter, and a bag of M&Ms. We divided the meal up, and set the M&Ms aside.

I forced myself to eat, but I could hardly stomach my third of the meal. Then Zeller took out his pack of cards and he and Santiago played a game of spades for the bag of M&Ms. Santiago won. Another jet, or maybe the same one, flew low but incredibly fast over the city. The air boomed behind it, but what could it do for us?

Santiago told us to get a few hours of sleep. When one of us woke up, he'd take a nap himself. Soon, Zeller was breathing easy. I told Santiago that I would watch the door. We traded places and soon Santiago was asleep as well. It was lonely with both of them curled up in their corners.

I told myself that a convoy was on the way. That they were cutting fast down desert roads toward the city, hurrying to rescue us. The cavalry was on the charge. But I knew it wasn't true. I knew that they wouldn't be coming into the city for at least two weeks. They'd wait until sufficient forces had gathered. For the time being, they'd expect us to help ourselves, to make our own way out, or to stay hidden until they arrived.

I tried to think of something happy, the way you're told to think of Hawaii and puppies if you're dying of hypothermia. I remembered the eyelashes. When I was in basic training, and then later when I first arrived at Fort Drum, a girl I once loved used to send me letters, and every time I opened one of them there was an eyelash hidden in the folds of paper.

Santiago awoke late in the afternoon. Not having anything better to do, he went looking for a fuck. He didn't say as much, but I could tell by the way he stepped out into the hallway. He strolled along slowly, then ran into a woman at the end of the hall. They didn't say anything, it was just a look, and he followed her back to her room. They shut the door and the lock clicked loudly.

I was smoking a cigarette in the doorway when Santiago returned from his adventure. Zeller was just waking up from his nap. Santiago said he gave the woman the pack of M&Ms.

"It's too bad we all don't have a pack," I said.

"That was the smartest thing I've done all day," he said.

"Nice," I said. "If only we had a truckload, we could fuck the whole city."

"You want her?" Santiago asked, a smile creeping across his face. "I'm sure she's game." Now he was really grinning. "You probably wouldn't have to offer her anything."

"No," I said, sickened at the thought of being where he had been.

"Zeller?" he asked.

"Why not?" replied Zeller. "You only live once," he added, picking up his 9mm.

"Sure thing," I said. "It's not like any of them have AIDS."

Santiago stepped out into the hallway and pointed Zeller to her room.

"I think we'll be all right," Santiago said as he returned to our room, "if we can just make it out of here." He went back to his bag and collapsed on the floor beside it. He rested his head on his rucksack.

"The fighting happened so fast," I said. "What could we do?"

"It's too late now," he said. "We're so far gone I can't feel myself anymore."

Early that evening I went downstairs to talk with Michael. I wanted to know what he really thought about our chances. I wanted to feel as if I had some control of the situation, or at least a better understanding.

We'd decided to head north, in the hope that the Army might still be waiting for us. If this failed, at least we'd be free of the city, and we could set out for the port cities. I needed a sense of hope. Even if it was all an illusion.

Michael was sitting behind his desk reading one of the books I'd given him, *The Strange Case of Doctor Jekyll and Mr. Hyde.* At the beginning of every month I was in the Army my mother sent me banana bread and another classic book to last the month. She was proud of her green-eyed boy as he plugged away at the world, trying to get to the heart of things. Michael put the book aside as I approached. I looked, but didn't see Cooper's 9mm anywhere.

"Sit down," he said, pointing at a couch to the side of his desk.

Dust rose as I took a seat, its particles faintly visible in the fading light of day. I felt as if I were underwater.

We sat in silence for a long time. He was waiting me out. I had the sense that he wanted me to say something first.

"Do you miss it?" I asked, "America?"

"Americans always think we miss America when we go home," he said.

"I'm sorry," I said, and truly, I was. "I just wondered."

He smiled and nodded. "I do miss it. But I also miss this place when I'm there. It's human nature."

"What's it like here?" I asked.

"Some days are better than others," he said. He looked at the 9mm in my hand. "You don't need that in my hotel. You're safe here for now. I'll let you know if it changes."

I nodded and set the weapon on the couch next to me, sliding it under my leg so I wouldn't forget it. The Army makes you pay for things that go missing.

"You're younger than the others," he said.

"I've been to college," I said. "I'm not the youngest." In fact, I was older than Zeller and Cooper.

"I liked college," he said. And then he asked, "Why are you here?"

"Money for school," I said. "But I'm here because they sent me. They give you a lot of trouble if you don't go where they tell you to go once you sign up. When I joined the Army I thought I was invincible. I was too young to think otherwise."

He nodded.

The front door was open. Wind blew sand in from the street, and a threadbare white curtain fluttered in the window across from me. There was sand everywhere. I couldn't keep it out of my mouth. I turned it around with my tongue and ground it between my teeth.

"What are people like here?" I asked.

"They're kind," he said. "And, how do you say," he took a deep breath and squared his shoulders, "proud." He smiled and nodded, rubbing his hands together. "It is often cruel though. People are desperate these days."

I watched him knead each hand in turn. I looked at my own hands and noticed several small cuts on the backs of them. I hadn't noticed them before. I ran my hand over the largest cut to see if it hurt.

Michael leaned forward and put his hands on his knees. Then he quickly rose. "Would you like a drink?"

One of the pamphlets they'd made us read before we were deployed said that if you were offered a drink or food you were to accept so as not to offend their hospitality, but you weren't actually supposed to eat or drink whatever you were given.

"Sure," I said.

He walked into a back room and brought back two bottles of what looked like a dark soda, along with two glasses. "You would like this place if you were here under better circumstances." He paused as he poured the soda. The liquid looked dark and heavy. He offered me the glass and I took it. I was a model of etiquette. Then he looked out the open door at the street and, nodding as if to emphasize his point, added, "I know you would have liked it here."

"How do you name your towns?" I asked.

He was still looking out at the street when I asked, but then he stopped and looked at me askance, a small smile starting on his face. "How do we name our towns? I don't see what you mean."

"I was just wondering what the name of this city means," I said.

"I don't know," he said. "I never thought about it. Where are you from?" he asked.

"Wichita, Kansas," I said.

He repeated the words slowly, delicately, giving them far more respect than most people did. Usually when I said the name of my hometown to a stranger they would repeat the word Kansas in some kind of strange drawl. Then they would tell me that I wasn't in Kansas anymore, as if they were the first person ever to say this. But when Michael said it it sounded exotic. I liked that.

"What does it mean, Wichita?" he asked.

"I don't have a clue," I said, and we both laughed. "We like to name our towns after the rivers that run through them."

He turned serious. "Does America know that we don't have any oil?" he asked.

"I don't know," I said, and I didn't. It had never come up in any of the briefings. "We're just here to help."

"It's hard to believe," he said.

"It's true," I said.

"There aren't many rivers here," he said. "You'll have a hard time renaming the cities if you stay."

I held the glass in my hand for a long time before forcing myself to drink. The soda was dark and syrupy and I sipped at it tentatively, slightly embarrassed.

═══ SIX ═══

WE DECIDED TO WAIT UNTIL AFTER MIDNIGHT BEFORE setting out. Hopefully that way most of the city would be asleep. Before going out into the night we stood over Cooper's body for a moment. In a way we had benefited from the way Cooper died. He showed us where the enemy was, and how they had the ground between us and the helicopters covered. Everything I'd ever heard about death came back to me again as I stood over him. Part of me wanted to stay, but we had to get going.

Shouldering my pack, I thought of all the choices it contained—almost every item in there could have been left behind. I hadn't brought a raincoat, but then who'd ever heard of rain in the desert? It felt good to be making our own choices, rather than having them be made by the sun or the city, or Cooper's needs. I was ready to follow Santiago, to show that I had faith in him.

Santiago tore off Cooper's name tag and the patches that identified him as a member of the U.S.

Army. He tore off his 10th Mountain Division patch, and he tore off the American flag on his left shoulder. He handed the scraps to me, but I didn't have a clue as to what he expected me to do with them. I held the patches for a moment, looking at the threads that hung from their edges where they'd been sewn onto Cooper's uniform. Then I put them in my rucksack.

"What religion was he?" Santiago asked. "I mean, he was really religious, right?"

"I knew when we got here," I said, "but I can't remember now." His feet extended beyond the edge of the mattress. And then I added, "I remember him saying he was a virgin because of his religion." I turned away from Cooper. "It will say on his dog tags."

Santiago looked from Cooper to Zeller and then to me. "Why don't you get them?"

"But you just touched him," I said.

"I touched his sleeve," Santiago said, "but I'm not putting my hand down his shirt." I waited quietly, hoping that he would change his mind. "All right," he sighed. He gingerly lifted the T-shirt under Cooper's BDUs and took the dog tags in his hand. "Islam," Santiago read. "What are you?" he asked, turning to me.

"Catholic," I said.

"And you?" he asked Zeller.

"Lutheran," Zeller said.

"What about you?" I said to Santiago.

"Unaffiliated," he said.

"What does that mean?" asked Zeller.

"It means I don't have a religious preference," he replied.

"I guess someone else will pray for him," I said. I didn't feel that we had the right. "We don't have to pray for him here. We'll have all the time in the world to remember him later, to say something meaningful."

"Probably," Santiago said.

Still, we stood around the body for a few minutes, and it felt as if we should say something. Finally, Santiago suggested that we find some other clothes for him. The owner of the hotel might get in trouble if they found a dead American soldier in one of the rooms. The body might even be desecrated.

But if we did take him out of his uniform, I said, we might void his will or his life insurance or something ludicrous along those lines. There were rules of engagement after all, rules that governed the way we lived, and there were probably rules that governed death as well. They didn't argue with me. We heard rumors and stories about things like that all the time. To those of us on the ground, it often seemed as if the government was always looking to avoid its obligations.

Santiago said that so long as all of us were staying in uniform, so should Cooper. I agreed with

him, trying to summon a sense of hope and meaning for what was ahead. If he was calling the shots
I wanted him to know that I believed in him. Even
if I didn't.

We walked downstairs to talk with Michael. He
said again that trying to steal a car in this town
definitely wasn't a good idea. He said the bus would
bring us better luck.

"Do you know how to get out of the city?" he
asked.

When we shook our heads, he waved us toward
the front door with a flick of his wrist, as if he were
tossing something into the trash.

"We need your car," Santiago said.

"You mean you're taking my car," he shot back.
He clasped his hands, rubbing them violently together. "I could have turned you in for the reward.
You killed two boys, it's all over the city. They're
looking for you, and they'll find you eventually,
even if they have to follow you home. They'll get
your names somehow and find you there. This is a
sick place."

He wasn't threatening us, really. He was simply
making an observation. We'd heard this before,
how trouble could follow you home from the war.

"They know you're still here because they saw
the helicopters turn back after they shot one of

them down." He was too angry to look at us as he spoke.

I wanted to tell him that what had happened with those two boys was an accident, and that I had nothing to do with it. But I didn't say a thing.

Then he said again that we'd never make it in a car. There were checkpoints and tolls through-out the city. We'd be dead as soon as they saw us. He said we could disguise ourselves as much as we liked, but when they spoke to us and we didn't answer they'd shoot us. "You'd have better luck taking the bus," he said. "People leave you alone when you ride on the trucks and buses here." He looked up from his hands. "Besides, I gave my car to a friend because I knew you'd ask."

"Where can we find a car?" asked Santiago.

"How will you know where to go?" Michael asked. "All the roads leading out of the city are mined. You don't just drive in a town like this. You have to know where to go."

"I've got a map," Santiago said. His confidence was obviously false. I'd seen the look before, when Santiago was drunk and trying to pick up a woman at the bar.

"Do you even know where your Army has gone?" Michael asked. "They're moving to a small city north of here to wait out the monsoon. Every-one here knows."

Santiago cursed under his breath, then turned and walked out the front door. Zeller and I followed.

We didn't know where we were going, but we knew we needed a car. Packs of dogs roamed the city, and they followed us for blocks on end. All the dogs looked the same: anxious, malnourished, and menacing. They were all dull brown in color, and when we stopped in an alley or to peek around a corner, they stopped as well, eyeing us distrustfully.

After an hour or so of searching and walking in circles, we found a car parked in an alley not far from Michael's. No one was around. There was a chain running from the steering wheel down through a large hole in the dash and then out through another hole in the floor of the car. There was no light in any of the buildings lining the street.

Santiago looked at the lock for a long time. The Army chained up its vehicles as well, but in this context it was unusual and unnerving. It was the most pathetic car in the world. The interior was all torn up, but still, on the end of the chain was one of the largest padlocks I'd ever seen.

Santiago told us to watch the street. To cover him. Then he fired at the lock, giving me a start.

Zeller and I turned to see what he'd done. There was a dent in the lock and a hole on the dash where the bullet had exited after ricocheting off the lock.

He fired another shot, blindly. I stepped away from the car, worried about where the bullet would end up. He fired four more.

The city was slowly awakening around us. Finally, Santiago pulled the chain out of the car. The Army had taught us how to hot-wire cars in survival school, so it should have been easy. But when Santiago reached in and pulled out a tangle of wires, I grimaced. It looked almost as if someone had stuffed the car with extra wiring to ward off thieves.

Suddenly a man came running up to the car, yelling as he approached. We had no idea what he was saying, but obviously he was the owner. He pulled at Santiago, trying to drag him from the car. Santiago kicked him in the knee. A woman came running to his aid. Santiago told us to stay where we were. The man struggled to his feet, tugging at Santiago and screaming incomprehensibly. He seemed to be trying to roust his neighbors.

Santiago swung and hit the man in the chest with the butt of his M-16. The woman grabbed Santiago's arm so he turned and kicked her in the midsection. She fell back onto the man. When the man stood and grabbed at Santiago's M-16, trying to wrestle it away, the weapon fired.

The man looked at us, wide-eyed and offended. The woman screamed into the silence left by the shot. The man fell into Santiago and Santiago held him up for a moment.

"Just give us the fucking car, you idiot," shouted Santiago. "You stupid fuck." Then he let the man fall to the ground. I saw a thick stream of blood seeping steady and strong from the side of his head.

Santiago trained his weapon on the man. The woman leaned over her husband, trying in vain to stop the bleeding. I was supposed to be watching the road behind us, but I couldn't stop looking over my shoulder at the man and the woman and Santiago.

"Please," she said, and then continued in another language. Then she repeated what appeared to be the only word she knew of English: "Please." She held the man's face in her hands. His eyes were emptying quickly.

Out of nowhere Michael appeared. He was breathing hard and his eyes were huge, almost inhuman.

"Tell them to give us the keys," I told Michael.

"Oh my god," he said.

"Please," the woman said again, then went on in her language.

"What the fuck does she want?" screamed Santiago.

Michael ignored the question. He looked from her to us, then grabbed ahold of my shirtfront and leaned into me with all his weight. It felt like he was trying to pull me to the ground.

People were gathering at the end of the alley. I didn't see any weapons, but their numbers were growing quickly.

Suddenly Santiago and Zeller took off running, but Michael clung to my shirt. His eyes were wide with fright and anger.

"Let go," I said, but to no avail. Suddenly a fairly large rock hit the side of my helmet. Several more landed around us. "Get off me," I screamed. Then I hit him in the face with the butt of my M-16. His nose opened and he crumpled to the ground, still trying to hold on to me. I started off after Santiago and Zeller.

I saw them ahead of me, running fast. People were crossing the street between us and I began to think I might lose them. I fired my weapon into the air and people scattered back behind walls and into doorways. Santiago and Zeller turned and slowed for me.

We ran until we couldn't anymore, then ducked into an empty building. It appeared to be an old hospital. There were bed frames and empty medicine cabinets scattered around.

"I didn't want to shoot that guy," said Santiago.

"I think I killed Michael."

"Why the fuck was Michael there?" I asked.

"I just meant to scare that guy," Santiago continued, "but he kept trying to take my gun. Goddamn it."

"I didn't mean to hurt Michael," I said.

Santiago took his rucksack off and dropped it to the floor. He turned to me, "Michael should have known better." He placed his helmet down on top of his bag. "Besides, I don't think you killed him. You definitely fucked him up though."

"Neither of you had a choice," said Zeller. He took his rucksack off and sat on it.

Some people just don't know when to leave well enough alone, I thought. Some people just can't avoid tragedy. He was stupid to try and stop us. We were desperate. I tried to convince myself that the man was a fool, an animal even.

My face and head were burning hot. I felt as if I was going to die from the heat. The sickness was on me again. Santiago made me lie on the floor and drink an entire canteen of water, but I couldn't keep it down.

"You're dehydrated again," he said. "If you get heat exhaustion we're through. We can't carry you and fight our way out. We all need to stay strong."

There was a stainless steel bathtub sitting upside down in a corner of the room. Santiago and Zeller flipped it over. Then Santiago took all of my gear and helped me into the tub. He handed me my

M-16 to hold. The metal in the tub was cool against my skin. Santiago handed me a full canteen.

Everything in the hospital was covered with sand. It wasn't the kind of place you'd want to come to for help. There were sandbags in the windows and glass crunched underfoot as Santiago and Zeller walked around the room opening cabinets and drawers.

I felt it all over again, the resistance and the hop of the weapon as it hit Michael in the face. I'd tried not to hurt him. He'd be fine. Just a bloody nose, maybe even broken, but nothing serious.

I lay low in the bathtub, my eyes closed, listening to Santiago and Zeller talking about our next steps. They were laughing about the absurdity of everything we'd tried so far.

"I don't think we're supposed to leave," said Zeller.

"But we can't stay," replied Santiago.

Then we could hear other voices. I couldn't understand the language, but it was clear that we weren't alone in the building.

"Easy," Santiago said. "Stay down, Stantz."

And then it was as if the world broke open from beneath us. And just as quickly it stopped.

Santiago leaned on the bathtub. He held a hand to his neck, but blood leaked out between his fingers, dropping on my lips and nose. I tasted blood as I tried to wipe it away.

"We've got to move," he said. Zeller and I helped him to a table, where Zeller applied our last compound press to the wound. Santiago's neck was a mess of flesh and muscle, but somehow the dark and serious veins were intact.

"We've got to get out of here," Santiago said, choking out the words. He was brightening the bandage quickly. He walked out of the room, leaving everything but his weapon. He left it all in a pile on the floor. I didn't want to carry it either. Nor did I want to leave it behind. Under no circumstances did I want them to know who we were. I looked at the bag for what seemed like a long time, but then I heard Santiago and Zeller going down the stairs and hurried after them, stepping over the two bodies in the hall.

We looked at the compass and decided to head toward the ocean. We knew it couldn't be far. A few people sat in doorways and gathered around fires that were burning in the streets. I couldn't understand why anyone would possibly want to have a fire in this heat.

Then we came out onto a long boulevard. Bushes and trees had sprouted in the middle of it. Everything was the color of sand, the color of the desert, even at night. A woman emptied what looked to be a bowl of piss and shit on the side of the desolate street. She watched vacantly as we passed.

=== SEVEN ===

I WALKED POINT FOR WHAT SEEMED LIKE HOURS. THEN we stepped over a sand dune and there was the sea, murmuring before us. Exhausted, we stood on the crest of the dune and looked back to make sure we hadn't been followed. There was nothing there.

The moon was a slit in the night, and there were stars everywhere. Dawn couldn't be more than a few hours off. For a moment my thoughts turned to Cooper, back in the hotel.

We collapsed into the sand. We were out of food and water. Santiago and Zeller checked their ammunition and discovered that they were on their last magazine. We divided up what remained, leaving us three full magazines each.

The wind was cool coming in off the ocean. I had goose bumps all over my body, but I was still on fire. I looked down at the shore, thick with foam.

"I guess we should just follow the coast out of the city," Santiago said. "Eventually we'll come across something. And besides, the helicopter pilots

99

like to fly up and down the coast. One of them is bound to see us."

It was true. In fact, I'd learned to fire a .50 caliber gun from a helicopter just a few weeks before as we flew along the edge of the ocean. When the crew chief tapped me on the back, I fired into the waves. Then we turned to fly back, following the same course, and Cooper fired out the opposite window.

We followed the coastline north, walking up from the shore only when rocks or other debris obstructed our path. After some time we came across what appeared to be a vast, abandoned shipping yard. There were old Russian fighter planes hulking in the darkness.

An old ship, half-submerged, peered at us from the ocean. It was the largest ship I'd ever seen, probably a tanker of some kind. I couldn't imagine a ship like that ever having been new. It looked as if it had been built to be abandoned.

We wandered around the rusting machinery until we found ourselves at the end of a pier, then turned back to look for a way out of this place. Finally, we found a road that looked to lead back down to the beach. When it switched back under the docks, we left the road and walked back onto the sand. The sand felt softer and deeper on that side of the pier, and in no time I could feel it draining the energy from my body.

We walked down to where the ocean rolled up and hardened the sand. My feet and pants were soon soaked. As we walked we passed a series of ramshackle dwellings; there were no lights on in any of them.

There was no end in sight. As we walked I tried not to panic. I considered giving up and sitting down where I was. Let the Army find me, I thought. Let them come to our rescue. They were probably rolling toward us even now, the heavy machinery humming, guns at the ready. They had to be coming, didn't they?

We came upon the dead end of a road that came right down to the shore. At its end we saw the back of a sign in the moonlight, and we walked up to see what it said. The lettering on the sign was illegible.

"How's your neck?" I asked Santiago.

"Can't feel a thing," he replied.

Santiago turned and walked back down to the beach, Zeller and I trailing along behind him.

"What do you know about ships?" Santiago said, asking no one in particular. Neither Zeller nor I responded. "I've always wanted to build my own boat," he continued. "One of those boats you can sail around the world. The only problem is that I don't know shit about boats. Still, I've always wanted to do that."

I couldn't imagine how he could possibly talk with his neck torn open like that. He should have been a memory by now.

Slowly the outskirts of the city gave way to run-down shacks and tents that looked like creatures crawling out into the night to die. Fires burned here and there in the alleys between them, and I could see the shapes of dogs passing low in the dim light. From where we stood, none of the fires appeared to be tended.

"Look at that," Zeller said, "there's a fire burning in a garbage can."

And sure enough, there it was, surrounded by a cluster of tents. We stopped and stared for a moment.

When I turned back around I could see lightning far out over the ocean. We stood there letting the wind wash over us. The night was slowly turning the color of mud.

"I guess that guy was right," said Santiago. "It really is going to rain."

We heard a few people yelling in the distance. Santiago said he needed to rest for a moment. He fell down in the sand, and was asleep almost immediately.

I looked at the wound on his neck by moonlight as best as I could. It was covered in dirt. Here and there, blood or sweat had pushed the dirt aside. The bandage was falling off, and it too was covered in filth. The mixture of blood and dirt was the color of tar.

"We need to keep moving," Zeller said. "It'll be morning soon."

"Just let him rest a minute," I said. "He's in bad shape."

"Do you think he'll be all right?" he asked.

"He'll be fine," I said.

"You're in charge if he dies," he said. "You got a plan?"

I nodded.

Then the yelling seemed to be getting closer. We tried to wake Santiago, but he didn't move. He was in the deepest sleep I'd ever seen. His chest rose and fell heavily.

The wind and the ocean played tricks with the sounds of the distant voices. One minute they sounded like laughter, then they were bitter and resonated with hate. Zeller said it was my turn to go see what was going on, that he'd stood watch at the hospital. He assured me he couldn't carry Santiago by himself anyway, so there was no way they were going anywhere.

"What if something goes wrong?" I asked.

He looked out over the ocean and shrugged. Then after a moment's silence he mumbled, "Fire a shot or something."

"Like in the movies," I said. I outranked Zeller, and I could have ordered him to go, but I decided not to. I knew it wasn't right to ask more of him at this point.

But I also knew that I wouldn't fire a shot if anything happened.

I moved out into one of the alleys, creeping along as if I were entering the voices themselves. When I had gone a mile or so from the shore, I took a knee in the wreckage of a small, bombed-out building, and peeked over the top half of what remained of a wall.

I saw the vague outlines of a man and a woman approaching me. A small crowd of seven or eight men and women followed along behind them, and they appeared to be agitated. Then they all stopped, some fifty yards away from me.

At first I thought it was a wedding, the way the crowd was following the couple. I concealed myself in the rubble and settled in to watch.

Suddenly a tall man stepped forward and slapped the back of the head of the man who had been walking ahead of the others with the woman. He staggered a bit, but stayed on his feet. The tall man hit him again, harder this time, and the couple started moving forward again. They held each other stiffly as they walked, like children playing at their first dance. But there was no music and the others didn't make a sound.

I could hear the ocean far off in the night, and then I watched as the crowd surrounding the couple grew more animated. They looked to be arguing. While the man and the woman walked ahead, the others erupted into recriminations.

I realized that the couple was in serious trouble. They had obviously done something terribly wrong. They looked down at the ground as they shuffled along.

Then the tall man hit the other man again and said something incomprehensible. The man who had been struck didn't move. He looked both exhausted and terrified.

I could see that there was only one other woman there in addition to the woman who had been walking ahead with the man, and at that point she stepped out to join her. The two women cowered away from the men.

The man who had been struck was now alone, and he looked frantically to the men surrounding him. When he began begging them for mercy, I knew that he was guilty of something unforgivable.

The woman who had stepped forward began arguing with the tall man. The other woman, the one who looked to be guilty of something along with the man, stood back away from the crowd, her head bowed. She was young, and I could see that she was the only one there who wasn't wearing shoes. Her feet looked tiny and delicate, and she appeared to be crying.

I could tell that the woman who had come forward was frightened by the way her body shook. She pleaded desperately with the tall man. She was the neighbor come out to help, or perhaps even a sister.

The tall man stood there with a tense expression, full of hate and fury. Suddenly it occurred to me that the man and the woman had committed adultery. And I knew just as well that this wasn't going to end well.

The tall man's body was rigid as the woman I took for his wife approached him. I wanted to call out to her, to tell her not to go near him. She reached her tiny hand out and touched him lightly on the arm. And with that he went into a fury.

He hit her once hard in the face, and then again as she was falling to the ground. Her head smacked the pavement. The man against the wall made a break for her, but two of the onlookers caught him and slammed him back.

I wanted to help. I didn't see any weapons, but this was a mob and somehow I knew they would kill me if I tried anything. Unable to act or to turn away, I whispered a prayer.

The tall man stomped on the young woman's chest and she coughed weakly. It was still dark, but I could see that blood was coming out of her nose and mouth as she tried to rise to her hands and knees. No one stepped forward to help her.

Then the tall man turned his attention to the man who had violated his honor. Several of the other men were holding the adulterer against a wall on the other side of the street, and the tall man ran across and hit him at full speed, crushing his forearm into the man's nose. His head snapped back and he collapsed to the ground in a heap.

In an instant the others set upon him, kicking him from all directions. At first he struggled to protect himself, but then he stopped trying and gave himself over to them.

After a few minutes of that, the tall man said something to the others and a friend handed him a knife. I saw the blade flash in the moonlight. The men surrounded their victim, who had struggled to his feet. I couldn't see everything, but it looked as if they were pulling his pants down. Then there was an awful scream, and the man fell to the ground again. The tall man kicked him a final time in the head, but he just lay there, not moving. They left his pants down around his ankles.

The woman was sitting up by now, trying to get her bearings. The tall man walked over and punched her in the face with the hand that held the knife. It was a move they'd taught us in basic training—punch and cut. Inflict as much damage as quickly as possible. The woman who had been trying to help ran off down one of the alleys. And then the man tore the poor girl's shirt open and went at her with the knife. He tired of it quickly, but there was no mistaking the damage.

After a moment of terrible silence, the men drifted off one by one. Finally the tall man turned and followed the others away, leaving the woman to die on the ground near her lover.

There was a little girl standing in the shadows a few feet away from me, waiting to see what I was going to do. I didn't know what all she had seen, but judging from the look in her eyes, it was more than a little. And when I stood to go, it looked as if she was planning to come with me.

I motioned for her to go away, but she wouldn't leave. She just stood there. She smiled at me and touched the sleeve of my BDUs.

"Go," I said forcefully. "Just go home now."

I walked back among the shacks and tents, side-tracking here and there so she wouldn't know where I was going. But each time I turned around, she was trailing along behind me still smiling. I took off running as fast as I could, but every time I stopped, there she was, laughing. She obviously thought it was all a big game. I was so tired I wanted to cry.

I took a roll of duct tape from my bag. I smiled at her as I wrapped it around her ankles, making it part of the game. Then I showed her how to hop. She laughed. And then I took off running. I stopped to look back a final time, and the look on her face as she tried to hop after me was painful.

I arrived back at the beach to find Zeller and Santiago sleeping. They were out in the open, clearly visible in what was left of the moonlight. And neither of them budged as I approached.

The sky over the ocean looked steely gray. Dawn was at hand. It would be Tuesday, or something near it. But that didn't matter much anymore.

I sat down beside them, drew my knees to my chest, and rested my head on the back of my hands. One of us should have stayed awake, but I couldn't bear to roust them. I closed my eyes and drifted off.

══ EIGHT ══

I WOKE UP BEFORE THE OTHERS, FEELING AS IF I'D emerged from another world. The sky was the color of mud, and barely distinguishable from the ocean. My head was heavy and my body felt awkward as I stood up. It was only then that I knew it was morning, and remembered where I was.

Santiago and Zeller woke up soon after, and groaned when they saw me pacing. We were out in the open again.

Santiago let out an awful sound as he sat up. His eyes were bloodshot and his face was dark with blood and sweat and filth. He licked and chewed at his lips, trying to wake himself up. He put a hand to his neck, winced, and pulled it away. His M-16 was slung across his chest, and he reached for it with the other hand.

A large sand dune rose behind us. We struggled to the top and looked out in the early morning light. Multicolored tents spread into the distance. Beyond them was nothing but desert, dotted sporadically with trees. A single road traversed the landscape, running north and south along the ocean.

"You have to be poor if you can't afford a house in this town," said Zeller.

"Do you own a house?" Santiago asked.

Zeller shook his head.

We walked back down the dune to the shore. After talking it over briefly, we decided to walk north, beside the road. My boots quickly filled with sand. The wind picked up and blew dust into our eyes. As I walked behind Santiago, I looked at his neck, covered with grime and blood.

For some reason I remembered an exchange I'd had with Santiago back at Fort Drum. He'd said to me, "You have a little Santiago in you, and I have a little Stantz in me." As if that was supposed to make us best friends.

After we'd walked for some time, we came across a man fishing in the ocean. He walked into the waves up to his waist, and cast the lure with all his might, as if he were trying to cast the city and all its curses right out of him.

Santiago sat down in the white sand. I turned and looked at the tents some distance behind us. There was no one else around, but we were still in the open.

I hadn't noticed it at night, but now I could see that there was garbage strewn all over the beach and bobbing in the shallows. The water smelled like raw sewage, much worse than where we'd slept. It occurred to me that the people who lived here probably dumped everything they had into the tiny creeks that emptied into the ocean. With all the sewage and trash, the air was heavy with flies.

The man caught three fish in a row, throwing them quickly to shore. "Jesus," Zeller whispered, "look at that."

As he came up out of the water to line his fish up on the shore before us, he looked at us with a smile. His mouth was spotted with rotten and missing teeth.

One of the fish was deformed by an old wound. It looked as if something had taken a bite out of it. The man held it up for us to see the deformity.

"What a beaut," said Santiago.

The man nodded in agreement. Then he turned and waded back into the water.

"God, my neck hurts," Santiago said. It had to be bad for him to even say that. Blood had dried under his nose and around his mouth. He stretched out and rested his head on the dirt behind him.

"We still have the kit," I said. "We're out of compound presses, but I could try to clean that wound and put some stitches in." I leaned over him to look at it. The bandage had fallen off to the side, and I could see the torn flesh. The bullet had somehow missed the artery, and there wasn't much of an entry or exit wound, so it would be relatively easy to close if he'd let me.

"Don't fucking touch it," he said. He pushed the dirty compound press back over the wound so I couldn't see it. "You two stay the fuck away from me."

After I had walked away, he pulled the bandage aside, took some alcohol out of the kit, and poured it over the wound. It hissed and bubbled.

The fisherman was still working the sea like a conjurer. Wherever he threw his line he seemed to catch a fish. He was pulling them out left and right and tossing them to shore. There was a nice pile in front of us.

After we'd watched the man fish for a few minutes, Zeller stood up and walked down to the shore. At first the man didn't see him, but then he did, and after a brief look of indignation, he watched silently as Zeller picked up a fish in each hand, then turned and walked back up to me and Santiago. The fish were hideously ugly, but Zeller stuffed them into his pack and we all stood to move out.

Having walked for some time along the shore, we came across a single abandoned building that had been largely destroyed. We sat in the rubble just up from the beach and rested. From this vantage point we could see the trucks that Michael had told us about. They'd speed by carrying dozens of people packed in the back of the truck, others packed in the cab, and often several more perched awkwardly on the roof. Most of these trucks looked to be heading back into the city.

We waited a long time before we saw one that was going in our direction. As it approached, we broke cover and waved for it to slow. The driver stopped and looked down at us, along with all his passengers.

"Hello," said Santiago.

The driver just stared back at us. The man sitting next to him leaned over and whispered something in his ear.

"Hello," Santiago said, louder this time.

"No." The reply came from one of the men on the roof. "The roads are closed for the monsoon." Then he said something we couldn't understand to the driver. The driver laughed and the truck lurched forward, slowly at first. Then it pulled away, the passengers all looking back at us.

Dejected, we walked back to the rubble. We waited there in vain for another hour or so, then walked back down to the beach and started out again. The sky was getting darker with each passing moment and the wind was picking up, swirling in off the ocean. I brought up the rear as we walked along the beach, leaving footprints that the tide would soon wipe away.

At some point we had walked beyond any sign of human habitation, and there was nothing but desert and ocean and sky. We walked up from the shore and out onto the road, so that we could get a good look at the desert. Gnarled trees no taller than a man dotted the horizon. Smaller bushes covered the sand as far as we could see. There was nothing promising about it.

Late in the afternoon, we stopped for a rest. Zeller reached into his pack and took out the fish. Santiago took out his bayonet and set about cleaning them.

Zeller and I searched for wood and kindling. We found some dried-out seaweed along the shore, and several dead trees. They were dry and brittle, and burned well once Santiago had a small fire going.

And then it started to rain. The water fell in huge drops, pregnant with filth. It wasn't the rain of home. Zeller put on his raincoat. He had grabbed Cooper's when we left the hotel, and now he gave it to Santiago. I pulled my poncho out and put it on.

"This might explain why there's no traffic on the road," Santiago said. "Probably won't see anyone out here for a while."

I set out my canteen cups and they filled quickly. The water smelled like rotten fish. I dropped a chlorine tablet in each of the cups, and handed one of them to Santiago. "We could get all kinds of diseases from this shit," I said, pointing to the fish and the water. But then nearly everything around us was a potential source of disease and death.

He laughed. "That's the least of my worries," he said. He looked down at the water as if there was something there for him to read. "My neck is totally fucked and you're worried about whether I should drink the water." He put the cup down and dug in his pocket for a cigarette. "It's insane," he said, looking out at the ocean.

The fire quickly went out in the rain. We tried to relight it under the cover of a tree, but it was really pouring now and the wind had picked up as well.

I looked at the raw fillets that Santiago had prepared. The fish smelled awful, but my stomach grumbled with need.

"What kind of fish is this anyway?" I asked.

"Fuck if I know," Santiago said. "It sure was ugly though."

"They smell like shit," added Zeller.

We stood there looking at the fish for some time, and then Santiago cut a small piece from one of the fillets. He held it under his nose for a moment, then extended his arm, breathed deeply, and shoved the chunk of fish in his mouth, swallowing it whole. Zeller and I stood there watching him.

"I've tasted worse," he said.

He cut off another piece and repeated the approach, but this time he gagged afterward. Then he raised his hand to the filthy wound in his neck, as if he could hold back the pain. I couldn't imagine anything worse than being wounded in that rain. The dirty water stinging the wound. The rot of everything it touched.

We had to eat to bolster our strength. I cut several small chunks off and swallowed them whole, washing them down with the foul water.

The rain and the wind kept up, and soon enough we were all shivering. I tied a T-shirt around my neck to keep the water off. My canteen cups were full again, so I poured the water into my canteen and dropped in another chlorine tablet.

Michael had said that it would rain for a month, and now I could imagine it. The aftertaste of fish and water was unbearable. Santiago handed us each a cigarette. We lit them in turn, cupping our hands so they wouldn't get wet.

Then we were sick, one after another. It seemed to last forever. When the spasms finally stopped, I sat down beside the road, rinsed my mouth out, and tried to compose myself.

"Somebody doesn't like us," said Santiago, sitting down beside me.

Zeller collapsed on the other side of me.

It was impossible to be sure in these conditions, but it seemed as if the light of day was fading.

"We'll stay here tonight," Santiago said, offering another cigarette.

I took out my poncho liner and tried to cover myself for the night. There were soft, muddy clouds low over the calm ocean, and above them ominous clouds the color of a freshly plowed field. Between these two layers a thin strip of sunlight was visible.

As I succumbed to exhaustion, I couldn't hear anything over the sound of the rain. I listened intently for helicopters, Humvees, or tanks, for any sign of our forces. But all I could hear was the rain.

I woke up during the night, my face wet with rain. For some reason I had a strong memory of a girl I'd kissed once as she cried. It was beautiful, her tears wet against my lips and my cheek. Softly, I spoke her name to myself, trying to recall the taste of her, trying to breathe it. *Lura, Lura.*

I turned to face the ocean. The wind was stale and rotten, and I knew there was no chance I'd get more sleep. My thoughts turned back to the grisly scene I'd witnessed the day before. To the mob and the pair of adulterers. And then there was the little girl, trying to hop after me as I ran away. How could anyone ever love me after something like that?

In the morning we stood and stretched in the rain. We sipped at the water in our canteens and joked about coffee and how it was Wednesday. "Hump day," Zeller said.

We set off down the road this time, tracing the shoreline.

Walking was much easier on the paved surface. We were careful to avoid the muddy potholes, in case they held a land mine. But we didn't want to lose sight of the ocean, so when the road turned away from it we returned to the shore.

After some time we began to approach what was clearly a ribbon of black smoke rising just beyond the next hill. We fanned out cautiously, clicking the safeties off on our weapons.

We waded through a slow-moving stream emptying into the sea, and then rounded a low rise and discovered the cause of the smoke. A semitrailer, gutted by fire, was smoldering alongside the road. The air smelled like burnt rubber. Sacks of rice were scattered about, bleeding their contents onto the earth. Zeller and I each picked up a half-empty bag and put it into our rucksacks. They were heavy.

We looked around cautiously as we moved through the wreckage. We looked for signs of what had happened, but there was nothing to go on. So we moved out again, heading in the direction that we hoped to be forward.

As we walked along the beach, Santiago brooded. "We'll have been gone for a week soon, and they have no way to find us. If we find a good place in the next few days we'll stop and stay there. They'll be looking for us up and down the highways. The rice will tide us over for a few weeks, maybe longer. We have to stay close to the road. Eventually they'll come back through here."

=== NINE ===

EARLY THAT AFTERNOON WE CAME ACROSS ONE OF THE strangest things I had ever seen: a hundred yards or so up from the shoreline was an abandoned caboose on a small stretch of railroad tracks that disappeared into the sand in both directions.

There was a wooden bunk-bed frame and a table inside the caboose, and a single lightbulb in a socket overhead.

"I'll take that bunk," Santiago said, pointing at the bed frame.

Zeller and I smiled. "It's all yours," I said.

We threw our bags into a corner, and quickly decided to stay there and wait out the rain. We'd use this shelter as a base camp of sorts, exploring during the days. We had enough rice to last a month, and we'd have the fish for at least the first week. Then we'd figure out something else.

We tore the bunk-bed frame from the wall and hacked it to pieces. Santiago told us to leave the table for another day. Zeller and I used our e-tools to break a small hole in the ceiling to let the smoke out.

The wood was thoroughly rotten, so it was hard to get a fire going. When we finally did, the smoke exited from the hole in the ceiling as well as two shattered windows. It must have made quite a sight from outside.

That first night we heard the sound of gunfire in the distance. I stepped out into the deluge and looked up and down the beach. There was nothing but the wind, coming in cool off the ocean.

We took turns pulling guard duty the first few days, though it was really just a matter of listening to the rain. I'd occasionally look out one of the windows, observing the slight changes in the light and longing for a sleep so deep that it would carry me home.

For meals we scrubbed the rice and soaked it in rain water. We boiled it in our canteen cups. When a thin film of dirt rose to the top of the boiling water, we'd skim it away. After we ate the rice we drank the water in which we'd boiled it, leaving the dregs and dirt on the bottom.

During the days we took turns exploring, walking for miles in every direction. But we never found anything other than stray dogs. As we returned to our camp we'd pick up gnarled branches and bits of deformed trees to use as firewood.

The rain was the only constant. And when it changed in texture or intensity, it moved all at once like a body in motion, like a flock of birds.

After we'd passed a few days in the caboose, I awoke one night to find Santiago sitting in the doorway, staring out at the ocean. A heavy rain pounded the roof. We never had enough wood to keep the fire going through the night, so I could barely see Santiago's features against the sky. I lay there on the floor, wrapped in my poncho liner, and watched as his lips moved and his face contorted with emotion. Then he stopped moving and lifted his head to listen to something. I shuffled around and cleared my throat so he would know that I was awake. When he turned toward me I asked him what was going on out there.

He turned back to the ocean. "Listen," he said, "children."

I couldn't hear anything but the rain.

I wanted to tell him it was all right. I wanted to tell him how easy it was to hear things out there. Angels, devils, whole armies passing by, a helicopter's rotor blades smacking at the waves and desert just out of reach, or everyone you ever loved moving past in a procession.

"I swear to god," he said, "I heard children playing outside."

I crawled away from my corner to look out the window across from me, hoping my eyes might see what my ears couldn't hear. I pushed aside the T-shirt covering the window. The wind was cool and damp on my face and sharp drops of rain pecked at my cheeks. I saw nothing.

I let the T-shirt fall back into place and crawled back to my resting place. Then I put my cheek down on the rough floor and closed my eyes.

"They're not there," Santiago said. "I looked too, but I couldn't see them. I'm losing my mind."

"Bullshit," I said. "You're fine."

"You don't hear them though, do you?"

"Just don't answer them," I said. "Don't think about it."

I rustled under my poncho liner, rubbing my hands to warm up. For a moment I could see Santiago's silhouette in the doorway. Then he turned his back to me, filling most of the frame. I could tell that he was agitated.

"The ocean's all wrong," he said. "It's out of tune." Then he stood up slowly, in obvious pain. He stepped out into the rain and turned his head skyward, opening his mouth to taste the rain.

I let him go. I curled into a ball to make myself small and warm. Still, I never got back to sleep. I just huddled there in the corner, trying to evoke Lura's voice. I tried in vain to picture her.

As the days passed we lost track of time. Sickness visited me again and again. Feverish, I moaned and kicked at the world as I slept. I saw ghosts and guardian angels and once even thought that I was home, in my father's house, in my room, the sunlight streaming in through the window to warm me as I woke.

Santiago's wound was covered with pus, but it looked a little better each day. In the morning and evening he boiled ocean water and poured it over the wound, cussing every time. "I'll outlive both of you yet," he'd say, grimacing. He chewed on his nails for hours, until his fingertips were raw and bloody.

We were constantly hungry. We had thrown the putrid fish away not long after arriving, and then all we had was the rice.

Outside, the world was drab and muddy. We were living in what seemed to be a perpetual twilight. The days and nights bled together, and I rarely knew on waking from some bad dream what time it was.

We often heard dogs barking in the distance. They scavenged the desert at night. After one of his nightly excursions, Santiago told Zeller and me that their tracks came to within a quarter of a mile from the caboose. He said they could do damage if they attacked us.

One afternoon I was working on the radio, thinking about how worried my parents must be. As the rain fell methodically, I thought about how news of our plight would be making its way around the world. When we returned, Charlie Rose and Larry King would want to talk to us. We'd be heroes.

"Do you have any cigarettes left?" I asked Santiago. He was sitting in the doorway again. He never seemed to sleep.

"I got a few I'm saving," he said.

I went back to working on the radio. I'd taken it apart to clean and dry it out. I knew a little about radios. They were my brother's hobby. Growing up, he always had four or five radios rising up from the boxes in which the parts arrived. We looked forward to reading the addresses to see how far they had traveled. He saved every dollar he made to spend on radios. My grandfather had been good with his hands like that, the kind of man that could hold his body steady long enough to solder a wire or a transistor into place. We often found him hunched over his worktable, magnifying glass held steady on a stand above a circuit board while one hand held the part in place, and the other went patiently about its work. I had none of that in me. I was clumsy, but at least I was trying.

Santiago cupped his hands and held them out to catch some rain. The air in the car was disgusting. It smelled like rotten fish, rice, Santiago's wound, and body odor. But as with anything, we were growing used to it.

Santiago turned in the doorway, bringing one foot in and leaving the other out. He closed his eyes and leaned his head back against the frame. His jaw was tight and his face had thinned out. His hair was longer than I'd ever seen it. He'd always kept it close, but now I could see gray mixed in with the dark growth.

There was sand in every crevice of the radio. It was ruining all our equipment, and soon it would ruin us.

"How many men did your wife sleep with before you?" Zeller asked Santiago.

"Hell, I don't know," Santiago replied. "I never asked." He stood and stretched his legs. "It doesn't really matter to me."

"You'd like to know though, right?" Zeller continued.

"Why?" Santiago said. He was pacing now. "You can't change it and it doesn't really matter anyway. So who cares?"

"I'm just asking," said Zeller. "I just felt like talking about something for a change." He was quiet then, but I could tell that he wasn't going to let it go. "After all, when you sleep with her you sleep with all the men she's been with before."

"That's a real theory you got there," said Santiago. I could see that he was getting angry.

I asked Zeller, "How many women have you been with?"

"Ten or eleven," he said.

"Is that Zeller talk or real talk?" asked Santiago.

"At least ten," Zeller replied. "But with one of them I was kind of drunk."

I thought of Cooper and his virgin girlfriend. He wouldn't have liked this conversation.

"Are those imaginary numbers?" asked Santiago.

"Look," Zeller said, "you may not care who your wife has fucked, but I'd like to know."

"Shut up," said Santiago. "Just shut the fuck up."

"Whatever," said Zeller, "she's probably fucking—"

Santiago was on him before Zeller knew what was happening. He had his hands around Zeller's neck and pushed him up against the wall of the caboose.

"I don't fucking care how many men your wife has fucked," Santiago said. "And if you don't shut the fuck up I'll fuck her too."

"Fuck you," snarled Zeller. Then Santiago let him go and Zeller stepped out into the rain.

Zeller didn't know when to stop, but Santiago was getting worse. He'd never been the most stable man, and between our losses, his wound, and the endless rain, he seemed to be breaking down.

After Zeller left, I stared at the pieces of the radio while Santiago paced. At one point he stopped in the middle of the caboose and hunched over as if he was trying to catch his breath. I wanted to ask if he was all right, but I didn't want to do anything to evoke his rage.

"I didn't mean to shoot that guy over his car," he muttered.

"He should have just left us alone," I replied.

"Or those kids," he added. "I just didn't know."

"There's no sense thinking about that now," I said. I didn't remind him about the dead we'd left at the stadium or the hospital.

"I made a real mess of it," he said, stretching to touch the ceiling. He hummed a few notes from a song I didn't recognize. "God, I haven't heard any music in weeks." He looked down at me and his eyes were moist.

"I better go apologize to Zeller," he said, and walked out into the rain.

The wind and the rain were heavy now, and in the silence left by the others I got to thinking about love.

For some reason I thought of the fact that I'd never really seen a woman nude before. I'd been with unclothed women before, but I'd never really seen a woman nude, walking around casually as if I weren't even there.

And then I thought about Lura again. I thought about her more the longer I was here, and I wondered if that meant I loved her. I hadn't even known her that well. We broke up a few months before I left, and since shipping out I had sent her a single letter with a single line: *Sometimes I think of you.*

My head hurt and my body shook. My pants were covered with shit and piss and blood. I tore at my scalp with my fingernails. I could never get the wind and rain out of my head long enough to make room for anything else. I shook my head, trying to clear it.

Lura had never responded to that letter, and I knew she never would. I closed my eyes and listened to the rain. I imagined her kissing me between the eyes. Then I sat back down in my corner and held my hands in my lap, rocking back and forth in rhythm with the world outside.

The rain had to stop sometime. Only a few more days, we'd say hopefully. We'd been eating nothing but rice for some time, and now the taste of it sickened us. We only ate when we really had to.

I finished the radio the following afternoon and inserted the batteries. It still didn't work. I tried all the tricks I knew, but there was no sound at all.

Santiago had been watching me work. Suddenly he stood up from his corner, walked over, took the radio out of my hands, and threw it outside. It landed in a puddle on the beach.

Zeller watched the radio fly and then turned back to Santiago. After a moment of unspoken hostility, he turned over and tried to get some sleep.

Santiago went out to pick up the radio and brought it back in. He looked over at Zeller sleeping in the corner and smiled. "Do you like me?" he asked. I thought at first he was asking Zeller, but then he turned to me.

"I don't dislike you," I said, trying to be funny.

He nodded vacantly, as if he were thinking of something else. "I have two babies," he said. "Did you know that?"

I said that I did. That I remembered them from the day we shipped out, when we were all waiting on the buses that would take us to Griffiths Air Force Base.

"They won't even remember me when I get back," he said. "They won't even know who I am."

"Maybe that's a good thing," I said. "You get a fresh start. Be a better father to them."

Santiago was the soldier civilians imagined when they thought of their army. A drinker when he wasn't on duty, and sometimes when he was. Strong, crazy even, but obedient when it came to orders.

That said, he was anything but stupid. I'd heard rumors that his rank had been reduced because he abused his wife and babies. But for all I knew they were nothing more than rumors.

He sat down beside me. His eyes were still bloodshot and his neck was all pus and scab. He smelled like rot. He put his heavy hand on the back of my neck briefly, then leaned back against the wall, pulled his knees to his chest, and dropped his arms to his sides.

"I don't even know where she is," he said. "They'll never remember me."

I couldn't remember how old his babies were. All I could see when I thought back to that day was a fleet of old yellow school buses. I remembered thinking how pathetic it was that the Army couldn't do better than the yellow school buses that stopped at railroad crossings. They stuffed us and our equipment, one eighty-pound rucksack and one M-16 each, into a space made for a child. And because they only gave us twenty-four hours notice, my parents and brother didn't come up from Kansas to see me off. Not having a wife or lover to wish me well, it all seemed so cruel. The two-hour ride to the Air Force base was hell.

Santiago shattered my sad reverie by slamming the back of his head against the wall. The moldy wood planks rattled. "If I die tomorrow they won't even remember me," he said. Then he crawled back to his corner, spread out beneath his poncho, and turned to the wall in search of sleep.

The next day Zeller and I talked about the movies we wanted to see when we got back to America. We decided to go to a theater and spend a whole day watching movies we knew nothing about. We'd pick them by nothing more than their title.

"I bet they'll make a movie about us," Zeller said. His face was thin and pale by now, and his eyes were sunk deep in their sockets, surrounded by dark shadows. He'd lost a lot of weight. We all had. I wondered what I looked like. Maybe like a hero.

"They'll make a movie about us," said Santiago, "made for TV."

We all laughed.

After a while Santiago said, "I wonder if they'll include the kids we killed?"

Zeller and I were silent.

"Do you ever dream about them?" Santiago asked.

"Why should we?" I said. "It doesn't matter anymore. We've been through all this before. We just have to get out of here and find the Army."

"You and Cooper used to talk about ghosts," said Santiago. "I heard you once."

"True enough," I said.

"We should have brought him with us," said Santiago. He was lying on his back in the middle of the caboose, staring up at the ceiling.

"Do you believe in ghosts?" he asked.

"No," I replied.

"I do," he said. "I think we're given a choice when we die. We can go up or down, or we can stay right here. Those who choose to stay here are usually just too angry to go anywhere else. Or maybe too sad, I guess."

"That was Cooper's theory too," I said, but in truth I wasn't sure anymore.

"I know," said Santiago.

"That's ridiculous," said Zeller.

Still on his back facing the ceiling, Santiago rubbed his forehead. I wasn't sure if he had even heard Zeller.

"Maybe in the end it doesn't matter," he said.

"I just can't believe it," Zeller said, obviously still stuck on the question as to where we go when we die. "After all, we all have a soul."

Santiago just lay there, smiling.

Suddenly Zeller stood up and walked to the doorway. "I'm going out," he said, and stepped out into the night.

"I like that," Santiago said. "It's good to believe."

"Maybe," I replied. I walked to the doorway and looked out over the ocean. I watched Zeller balance himself on one of the rails of track that led nowhere.

Santiago reached out and took my poncho liner and wrapped it around himself. "Just take this back if you need it," he said.

"I will."

I walked out into the rain. It felt refreshing for a change, as if what I smelled and tasted when it began had been washed away. But it still didn't taste like the rain I remembered from home.

After a few minutes, I walked back into the caboose and stoked the fire with a stick. Sparks and ashes rose and snapped.

Then it was eerily quiet. The rain had stopped for the first time in countless days.

Santiago and I stepped out of the caboose. Zeller was there too, and we all stood and looked to the sky. A thunderclap sounded in the distance, but sure enough, there was no sign of rain.

"We move out tomorrow," Santiago said. "We've already been here too long."

═══ TEN ═══

THE NEXT MORNING WE ROSE EARLY. WE CLEANED AND oiled our weapons in the gray light of dawn, and after a breakfast of rice gruel, we moved out. For no good reason, we felt strong again.

We decided to take the road. If the Army really was looking for us, we thought, they'd find us on the move. They had to be making their way toward the city on the road. We talked about what it would feel like riding into the city at the front of that hard, sharp edge.

I walked point and we marched along like professionals. As the morning moved along, we passed a number of people traveling along the road in the same direction as us. We wondered if they were leaving the city because they were afraid of what would happen when the Army and the clans met on the streets of the city. But they didn't pay much attention to us in any case. Our uniforms were filthy and in tatters, and by this point we were hardly recognizable as Americans. We were simply men in rags with weapons.

The diet of nothing but rice had left us weak, and after the initial high we stopped often to rest.

We'd been walking for several hours when we came across a truck mounted with an anti-aircraft gun on the side of the road. A crowd of people had gathered around, but they dispersed as we walked into their midst, leaving the truck to just a few armed men.

"Let's just keep walking," Santiago said under his breath. His wound had scabbed over, but it was still swollen with infection. "Don't look at them, just keep walking. These guys don't want a fight." As we passed, the armed men smiled at us.

Then we heard another truck approaching, moving fast. It slowed as it passed alongside us, and the men in it called out to the armed men. Then I heard the low thump and slap of helicopters' rotor blades. I turned toward the sound in order to gauge the direction and the distance.

The armed men were suddenly serious, and they climbed back into the truck. Once they were aboard, they sped off. One of the men quickly manned the anti-aircraft gun.

The other truck followed, and one after another the two of them turned onto a side road that went off into the desert. We stood where we were and

watched. I could tell now by the sound of the helicopters that they were Apaches.

When the helicopters came into sight we waved
our arms to get them to notice us. Suddenly, the
trucks began firing at them and the helicopters fired
back. I could hear the whine of the big .20 calibers
spinning on the helicopters' snouts. Rounds tore
into the dirt around both of the trucks, and before
long one of them burst into flames.

The first truck we had come across was un-
damaged as of yet, and it moved off slowly, back in
the direction of the main road.

The other truck was burning up quickly, and I
could see a few bodies littered about. A thin wire of
black smoke climbed into the sky.

As the surviving truck accelerated toward us, we
stepped well off the road to give it plenty of room
to pass. But just as it did so the helicopter launched
a rocket. The truck exploded into a fireball. Before
I knew it I'd been knocked off my feet by the blast.

My head throbbed, and as I struggled to get up I
realized that there was another body on top of me.
I could taste blood, but I couldn't hear anything
other than a loud ringing. I felt someone kick my
head and I tried to grab the foot. Another kick, and
then another.

I tried to free myself from the body on top of me.
Someone punched the side of my face and pried the
M-16 from my hands. Then I felt someone trying

to take my 9mm out of its holster. I finally pushed the body off and drew my 9mm from its holster. My rucksack felt incredibly heavy, and I struggled to stand up.

There was fire everywhere. The body I'd pushed aside had left a sticky mess of skin on my uniform and hands, but the man's face was unblemished. He probably never knew what hit him.

Black smoke scrolled around me. People appeared out of the smoke and then disappeared just as quickly. They were looting the bodies, fighting each other for the possessions of the dead. I fired a shot into the air. I couldn't hear it, but I felt the weapon's kick.

Several men ran at me, wanting the 9mm. I shot the first one that reached for it. He was a little old man. The others stopped. I pointed the 9mm at them and they slowly backed off.

The truck was burning behind me; I could feel the heat. I coughed and choked. I didn't see Zeller or Santiago. I went from body to body, calling out for them.

The looters left me alone and went about picking over the others. They dug through the flaming debris of the truck and pulled the men out, stripping their bodies of anything of value. Suddenly the anti-aircraft gun started burping its rounds off randomly. It must have been set off by the heat.

An old woman took my arm, hurried me down the road, and helped me into a ditch. There were several people there, and one of the men was submerged to his waist in standing water.

The old woman took off my helmet and wiped blood from my face. Then she showed me the rag, put it in my hand, and pressed it to the side of my head as a reminder.

I asked, gesturing, if they'd seen my friends. They looked at each other, confused. "The other two," I screamed. A man directly across the ditch from me smiled strangely.

The old woman wrapped a young girl in a wet dress and said something to the others. Suddenly everyone except for the man across from me stood and left. When I stood to go, the man stood as well and put his hand on my shoulder, obviously hoping to use me as a kind of crutch. He looked disappointed when I tossed the rag aside, put my helmet back on, and stepped away from him.

Rounds cooked off from the burning truck and bullets rang overhead with weak whistles. The ammunition can in the truck exploded and one of the rounds landed next to me, green and glowing.

I climbed up out of the ditch and walked back into the burning wreckage, looking for Santiago and Zeller. They must have been killed in the blast, I thought. You never know where to stand in a war.

The helicopters hadn't seen us; they wouldn't have fired if they had. But the fact that they had been here meant there was probably a base nearby.

I couldn't find Zeller or Santiago anywhere. It was as if they had vanished. Not knowing what to do, I stood there looking at the corpses littering the earth around the truck for what seemed like forever.

When I finally composed myself, I realized I was all alone. The smell of burning flesh and metal drove me from the road, and I stumbled off into the desert. I knew that I should be careful, but I had no idea what to look out for.

As I walked, I tried to remember my survival school training. Santiago would have told me not to think so much. That was all I could remember. I hadn't really listened to the rest. I hadn't really cared. At the time I never would have imagined I'd have to go it alone.

Dead tired before long, I found a rock and sat down. I turned back and saw the road in the distance. I took out the clip in my 9mm. Just five rounds remained. Somewhere along the way I'd lost my rucksack, and with it the other two clips of ammunition.

I thought of the man I had shot on the road, and shook my head. I didn't need that memory now. I'd been threatened, after all. I was in real danger. But it didn't matter anyway.

I thought again of Santiago and Zeller. I watched the road for a long time, hoping to catch sight of them.

Puddles of water spotted the desert, but other stretches seemed very dry. The sun came out, casting its uncaring light on my blackened boots and pants. I slapped my legs and watched the reddish dust rise.

I had minor wounds in several places, and the blood had dried and turned dark and crusty. I took off my helmet and wiped my face with what was left of my sleeves. Then I put my helmet back on and started walking, turning back often to look for Santiago and Zeller.

I walked for hours without seeing anything, until eventually I came across a dirt road that looked to lead back toward the city. I thought for a moment of heading in that direction, but decided against it.

I was in bad shape when I heard the unmistakable sound of a whistle and stopped, bewildered. It was only then that I saw a small compound less than a half mile ahead of me. Suddenly an American soldier stepped from behind a small tree and grabbed me. He guided me back to a spot hidden from the house by a sand dune.

"What the fuck are you doing?" he said. "Trying to give away our position?"

When I looked around I saw several more soldiers, their faces painted in camouflage. They wore bushes as hats and had sticks on their shoulders, and they looked to be pissed off.

"Jesus Christ, man," one of them said, "didn't you see us waving at you?"

"No," I replied.

"What the fuck happened to you?" These men were obviously used to getting the answers they wanted.

"I got lost," I said. "With the others." I pointed in the direction of the main road along the ocean. "I think they're dead."

"You look like shit," one of them said. "A big shit sandwich."

They all laughed. I could tell they'd heard that before.

"Look at your head," another one said.

Then an additional soldier, his face painted black, appeared out of nowhere. "I don't think dumbass gave us away," he said. He hated me already, I was sure.

"You look like shit," he added, leaning close to look at my leg. "Jesus Christ," he said, pointing at what looked to be a long gash that cut through my boot and into my ankle. "You should put something on that."

"Yeah," I said, "I've been meaning to."

He nodded and looked at the wound on my head. "Why do you think your friends are dead?"

"I looked everywhere but I couldn't find them."

"Leave the Humvee but go look for them," another one said. "On the road?" he asked me.

I pointed at the black smoke far in the distance. "You didn't hear the explosion?"

He shook his head.

"We're focused on this place," said one of the men. "We're going to tear this fucking house down. Want to help?"

"I'd like that," I said. "Do you have anything to eat?"

The man who had grabbed me took out a medical kit. "I'm Mark," he said. He rolled my shirt sleeve up and gave me an IV.

"That's Clip," he said, pointing at the man who wouldn't shut up. "Candid," he said, pointing to one of the camouflaged men. "Jordan," he said pointing at another one. "And Simon and Nichols just took off for your friends."

Mark cut the laces from my boot, slid it off, and rolled my pant leg up. He picked pieces of the pant leg and other debris out of the cut. I couldn't feel a thing. When the wound was cleaned, it didn't look that bad. There was a long gash, but it was all surface. Then Mark said that my head could use some stitches.

, Jordan gave me an MRE. A ham slice, my least favorite. It was the kind of meal you saved for unwanted guests.

I put my boot back on and Mark handed me a roll of duct tape. I wrapped the tape around the boot until I was sure the boot would stay on.

"What's with the house?" I asked.

"Who the fuck are you?" Clip asked.

"Joshua Stantz."

"No." Mark was still sitting next to me. "He means who you with?"

"10th Mountain," I said. "You?"

"Recon," he replied.

"How'd you get out here?" Clip asked. The others had turned from observing the house to listen.

"Leave him the fuck alone," Jordan said. "You're in that group that went missing, right?"

"Alpha Company," I said. "Maybe I could use your radio?"

Clip shook his head. "Radio silence, Candy." Now they were giving me nicknames. "We're in the thick of it here." And with that he smiled.

"Who's in charge?" I asked.

They all looked at Mark.

"If you could just call and get me a ride out of here," I said. "I could even walk back and meet them somewhere. I could tell them about the others."

"I'm sorry," Mark said. "Orders are orders. I can't

break the silence. Anyone could be listening. Believe me, I would if I could."

"What if I were dying?" I asked.

"But you're not," Mark said, shaking his head. "Sorry."

"How far are we from the city?" I asked.

"About thirty miles."

I wondered about the abandoned caboose. The weeks that had passed, and all the dead. I added it up. We sure hadn't made it very far.

I pecked at my MRE. "Who's in the house?"

"One of the warlords," Mark said. Then he leaned back and pulled his Kevlar over his eyes. "Wake me up in a few hours."

Jordan pointed me behind a tree for cover. I asked for some water, and they handed me a canteen. There were flies everywhere. They crept at my eyes, my ears, and my nose.

"The warlord has some sheep," Jordan said. "They come out and meet us in the morning and in the evening. We give them food that's drugged so they don't care if we slip in among them. We're going to use them as cover when we go into the compound. When they go back inside, we'll move with them."

"Sounds like a hell of a plan," I said. "Drugged sheep food. Where's the main column now? I'm sure I could just walk back there."

"Can't let you, Nancy," Clip said, eyeing me. "You're with us now. If you get caught we've been wasting our time. I hate wasting time. Seems stupid."

After another hour or so, Simon and Nichols returned. They hadn't seen Zeller or Santiago, but they had seen the wreckage and quite a few refugees fleeing the city. They said they'd seen a number of burnt bodies. Crispy critters, they called them.

"You're in, right?" Jordan asked. "Payback time for your fucking compadres? It'll be easy, anyway," he added.

"Where's your M-16?" Clip asked.

"I lost it."

"Shit happens," he said. "Though you'll be in some really deep shit for that one."

"They'll take it out of your paycheck," Simon explained, "and those weapons are expensive."

"More than you make, Susie," Clip added, smacking me on the back.

I rolled over onto my side and slid my helmet over my face to fend off the flies. I closed my eyes and drifted off to sleep.

===== ELEVEN =====

THE THROBBING GASH ON MY HEAD WOKE ME. THE LEG wound itched as well. There were flies under my helmet, crawling along the wound. I took it off and rolled over onto my back. It was hot. Jordan handed me a wet cloth, and I folded it across my forehead.

"You look like you could use it," he said.

"Have some Kool-Aid," Clip said. He handed me a water bottle filled with orange Kool-Aid. It was so sweet I almost threw up. I hadn't tasted anything sweet in a long time.

"They're worked up about something," Mark said, looking through his binoculars at the house.

"Do you think they've seen us?" I asked.

"No," Mark said. "They don't get out of the compound much. There is only one guard, and he's usually asleep."

"Look at this motherfucker," said Jordan, kicking a tarantula the color of sand into the center of the circle.

I stood quickly. Those things could jump. Everyone was on their feet, stepping away from the spider.

"Holy shit," said Jordan nervously. "Look at the size of that thing." It was the largest spider I'd ever seen.

Jordan threw his knife at it but missed. The handle of the knife brushed the spider, and it moved around frantically. Clip prevented its escape with a long stick.

Then Mark threw his knife at it and missed as well. Candid tried and he missed too. Finally, Clip smacked it with the stick and it popped up into the air.

"Holy shit," said Jordan.

Clip walked over and stabbed his bayonet through the tarantula's fat body. Its legs churned, but the blade was stuck firmly in the ground. When Clip pulled the blade from the ground, the spider was still on it. Then he took out a lighter and lit the spider's legs on fire. It quickly curled into a ball.

"Stop fucking around," said Mark. "That's all we need is for your stupid fucking shit to give us away." And with that he went back to watching the house. The sun was going down, so he used a hand to shade the binoculars. Then he put them down.

"What are they doing?" I asked.

"Sitting around after dinner," he said. "After that

they usually go off and fuck a few women and fall asleep. Hell of a life."

"You get laid while you were in town?" asked Candid.

I tried to ignore him, but he stared at me, waiting for an answer. The others turned to see what I'd say as well. "No," I said finally.

"There are some gorgeous women in this country," Clip said. The others laughed at this, but I wanted to tell them there were.

I slept for a while, and then Clip woke me by pounding firmly on my helmet. "You're doing the kickin' chicken," he said. He slapped me on the helmet again.

I took it off. I couldn't remember ever having been more tired. The wound on my head was throbbing. Clip slapped my head again, laughing. I wanted to kill him.

"We move in an hour," said Mark.

Everyone grew quiet.

"We heard you killed some kids," said Clip. "That's what they're saying back at camp. I thought you said you didn't kill anybody."

"I didn't fire a shot," I said.

"Who cares?" Mark said, turning toward me.

"I think we should know who we're helping here," Clip said.

"What've you got for us, Stantz?" said Jordan.

"It doesn't matter," Clip said, "I'm just asking."

"I didn't shoot anybody," I said.

"It doesn't matter anyway," said Mark. "Leave him alone."

Clip put a hand on my shoulder. "I'm sorry. What happens here stays here, right?"

"Sure," I said. It made this whole thing sound like a vacation.

"Bad things happen in threes," Clip said, to no one in particular.

"That's not true," I said. "Bad things just happen."

Jordan had fallen asleep sitting up. His head listed heavily from side to side. Simon and Nichols snuck out to check our perimeter and the perimeter of the house.

"Tell me about the last woman you were in love with," said Clip. He looked at me from under his helmet, and his brown eyes were bright for a moment, as if he was remembering his own.

"What?" I asked.

"It's a game we play," he said. "To pass the time."

I didn't want to tell them about the last woman I'd loved. I didn't want them to know anything about me, and especially not that. Not a glimpse, not a whisper, not a sordid desire. It felt profane to even think of her in this place. Those memories were sacred.

"Why the last love?" I asked. "The last love never seems to matter as much as the first."

"Whoa," said Clip sarcastically. "We got us a real fucking genius here." Clip and Mark laughed.

"No really," Mark said, "who was the last woman you fell in love with?" He wanted an answer.

I lied. "Amy." She was the first girl I loved. The first girl I ever kissed.

"Amy what?" Clip asked.

You couldn't talk to men like these about women. Men like Clip carried pictures of their girlfriends in lingerie, pictures to be savored quietly at night. But in fact they displayed them to everyone. I saw it all the time.

"Amy Williams," I said.

Mark and Candid were watching the house intently. The sun was almost down, and the sky above it was bursting into color.

"She lives in Boston now," I said.

"You from Boston?" Clip asked.

"No," I said. "Kansas."

"Well," Clip said, "you ain't in Kansas no more." They all laughed. It was the funniest joke they had ever heard.

"She from Kans-ass, too?" Clip asked.

"No." But then I was talking about Lura, and I immediately wished I weren't. "I don't know where she's from originally. They moved around a lot. She's in college. Acting, or something like that."

"Nice," Mark said, turning back to look at me. It was as if this elevated me in his eyes, as if it really mattered where we were from and whether we'd ever been in love.

"She's pregnant now," I added. Which was true, and again I wished that it weren't. I had never even told Cooper or Santiago this. "But it's not mine." I wouldn't have added that if it really mattered.

They all nodded. Stories like that were common in the Army. A classmate of hers got her pregnant, at some school out east.

"That's fucked up," Clip said. "I feel for you."

"Maybe there's still a chance you'll be with her," he added. "If you want one."

"I don't know," I said.

Then Clip reached into his shirt pocket and took a picture out. He handled it carefully. "Lucy," he said.

She was pretty. She was wearing a green sweater, and I could almost smell it. I nodded lightly. Red hair, freckles, she could have been anyone's girl. But she was his, and I liked that. I handed it back to him. "She's beautiful."

He took the picture back and smiled. "I know."

Simon and Nichols returned from patrol shaking their heads. Mark looked at his watch and then picked up the radio and made a call. We all watched him.

He hung up the receiver. "He's not here."

That was all. That was the message.

"The warlord," Mark explained. "He's not here. The Army is moving into the city tonight and we're to take the compound. We'll flush him out, then we'll find him and crush him."

The others were excited. The adrenaline was pumping, you could see it in their eyes.

"You're with us now," said Mark. They all nodded. "We'll get you back to your company when it's over. Now we take the compound."

"Maybe I could use the radio real quick?" I asked.

"That was it," Mark replied. "That was the one window for our call." He turned back to the house.

"I just want them to know I'm still alive," I said. "I should tell them about the others."

"I'm sorry," Mark said, "but you're part of our mission now. Yours is done and you made a mess of it. This is your chance to make it right."

"Sure enough," I said. "But I'd just like my parents to know I'm all right."

Mark shook his head. They set about putting on more camouflage. When they handed it to me I passed it along to the next man.

I asked if there were reinforcements, if there was anyone to support us.

"We have everything we need right here," said Clip. The others nodded in agreement.

When darkness had settled around us, we crawled out into the desert, heading toward the compound. They used their NVGs and their infrared scopes, while I simply crawled with my cheek to the earth. When the guard rounded a corner and stepped out of eyesight, Mark gave the signal and we stood and ran to the sheep. Mark and the others gave them the drugged feed they'd mixed back at the base.

Suddenly Mark whispered to us to get down. The guard had just walked back around the wall surrounding the house and was in sight again. We crouched among the sheep.

When the coast was clear Mark led his men forward with the sheep. I fell back to the rear, and then turned and sprinted to a low line of trees, half expecting to be shot from behind.

I found their camp a short distance from the trees. They'd taken the radio, but left the rucksacks, so I dug through them and took another clip of 9mm ammunition.

Just as I was leaving, gunfire and a series of explosions broke out in the compound. Sheep and men were running in every direction. Tracers from an AK-47 arched up into the night sky and disappeared among the stars.

I hurried off into the night to look for their Humvee. They had a radio, so I knew they could always call for another one. If I made it back to camp and anyone asked me why I stole the vehicle, I'd simply say I was crazy. People got away with that kind of thing all the time.

I stumbled around for a few minutes and then tracers broke the night open in front of me. Someone was close, firing at me with an AK-47. I hit the dirt and crawled into a thicket. I fired my 9mm at the spot I thought the shots were coming from. I knew I hit my target by the way the night seemed to stop.

I was sure the enemy had me surrounded and was now closing in for the kill. They'd been waiting for us the whole time.

Then I heard a familiar voice. "Fucking shit." It was Zeller. He screamed, firing wildly into the night.

I wanted to yell out, to let him know I was there. But I didn't want him to know that I was the one who had shot him.

"I'll fuck you up, motherfucker," Zeller shouted in my direction. He fired a few more rounds, then stopped as if he'd run out of ammunition.

I waited about a minute or so, listening to his curses, the wind, and the fighting in the background. But I knew I needed to move, so I jumped up and fired a few rounds into the earth. "Zeller," I screamed.

"Stantz?" he called.

"I got him," I yelled. I put a few more rounds into the earth to make it seem as if I were finishing the job. "I killed him." There were tiny pocks in the earth where the bullets had hit.

I ran over to Zeller and dove down next to him. "We need to get out of here. There's a group of American soldiers fighting in the compound over there. This is their Humvee. I say we take it and get you to a medic. The Army is advancing on the city. We'll meet them along the way."

"Santiago will be back in just a minute," he said. I could see that his face had been burned horribly in the explosion back on the road. One of his BDU sleeves was missing, and much of the skin had been melted off his arm. Sand spotted the flesh that remained.

"Santiago headed for the fight to see what's going on." Zeller was having trouble breathing. "We looked for you. What happened?" He held both hands over his abdomen. I tried to move them away to see if there was anything I could do, but he wouldn't let me lift them from the wound.

Then Santiago called out from the darkness. "Zeller?"

"It's Stantz," I called back.

He found us and took a knee next to Zeller. "What the fuck?" he said. He too reached to take Zeller's hands away from the wound, but he still resisted.

"Someone shot me," Zeller said, turning to Santiago. "Stantz got him though."

Santiago looked at me. "Where is he?"

I pointed in the direction of the compound, then told Santiago about the advancing Army and how we could meet them and find a medic if we just took the Humvee and found the road again.

"What happened to you back there?" asked Zeller. "We couldn't find you."

"I don't know," I said. "I looked for you for a long time."

"Let's get him in the Humvee," said Santiago. There were heat blisters from the blast all over Santiago's face and hands, and his skin had been darkened by the smoke and soot.

We lifted Zeller together and carried him a few feet before we stumbled and fell. There was lots of blood, and he was too heavy for even the two of us. He wouldn't let go of his wound, so we each reached under one of his arms and dragged him to the Humvee. We put him in the backseat.

"You drive," said Santiago, and climbed into the back with Zeller to try and work on the wound.

I left the headlights off because I didn't want any trouble. We needed to find help for Zeller. In the light of the stars and the moon, I tore off, heading in what I thought was the direction of the road.

As we drove, Santiago asked Zeller what he would do first when we got back to America.

Zeller said he wanted to sit in his shower for a few hours.

"That sounds good," said Santiago.

We were lost in no time. It was our curse. All I could see in any direction was sand dunes and darkness. I followed flat stretches of the desert until encountering trees or gullies or dunes. When I felt sure that we were not in imminent danger, I turned on the headlights. As we drove, I imagined the Army tearing across the desert.

We bounced along violently for an hour or so, searching for the road. Each jolt brought a low moan from Zeller. The Humvee's engine started smoking and the oil pressure dropped.

"You stupid fuck," I said, cursing him under my breath. Why had he shot at me, and what was he doing with an AK-47? Once when I turned to look over my shoulder at the two of them, I saw Santiago whispering into Zeller's ear. When Santiago saw me looking he paused.

After what seemed like hours, we drove over a small rise and I saw the dark of the ocean before us.

The horizon was just beginning to show the first light of dawn.

"Turn right," said Santiago from the back. "Just drive along the ocean toward the city. There has to be an advance party out here somewhere with a medic that can help him."

I quickly found the road we'd been walking along before. I flew down it, hitting potholes without fear of land mines. Refugees heading north appeared at intervals and watched us as we sped past. One man waved his cap to us.

The Humvee's engine finally cut off and the vehicle slowed until we rolled to a stop.

"He's dead," said Santiago.

"I know." I stepped out of the Humvee.

I saw two adults and a child approaching us in the distance. It must have been a family.

I tossed my helmet into the driver's seat and picked up my 9mm. Sand was blowing in off the desert. I stood there leaning against the hood of the Humvee, the 9mm at my side.

Then Santiago said softly, "I told him. I told him everything."

"Told him what?"

"That you killed him," he said. He was still sitting beside Zeller in the backseat.

"You didn't have to do that," I said.

"He didn't know it was you," Santiago said. "I heard him fire that AK, then it was a 9mm. I knew he'd lost his, which meant it had to be you."

"You could have left it alone," I said. "He didn't need to know."

"But I knew it was you," he said, looking off into the distance.

"Why didn't you just let him blame it on this place?" I said. "He fired at me with an AK-47. How was I supposed to know it was Zeller? And what was he doing out there anyway?" I leaned against the warm hood of the Humvee. "Where the fuck did he get an AK-47?"

"We stripped it from the dead," Santiago said. "From those we killed on the road."

"He could have called out before he fired," I said. "He could have killed me. You didn't have to tell him. He would have just blamed it on this place."

"We made a mess of this whole thing," said Santiago. "And I'm sick with it."

The family walked by, eyeing us carefully. The man smiled, but the other two were more wary, and all three of them made a wide circle around us. Their bright clothes stood out against the dull tones of the desert.

Santiago wiped the blood on his hands on Zeller's pants, and stepped out of the Humvee. I still had the 9mm in my hand. Santiago took his M-16 and slung it over his back. He felt to make sure that his

9mm was still in its holster. He was covered in dirt from head to toe. He was so far gone I didn't even recognize him anymore.

Whitecaps spotted the ocean before us. I couldn't feel a thing. It was almost as if I were watching the moment from above. I could see Zeller in the backseat, his head to the side as if he were waiting for another secret.

Santiago stepped in front of me. "There's no forgiveness for something like that," he said. There was something menacing in his voice.

"I'm going home," I said, too tired to move anymore.

"We'll never get right with the world again," he said, fingering the safety switch on his M-16.

"You have babies at home," I said. I didn't want to die there. Not after all we'd been through.

He looked out over the desert. "I'd love to go to the mountains. I know they're out there beyond the horizon." He sat down next to me, right on the road. "I bet they're beautiful."

In the first light of day a low dark cloud appeared on the road behind us. It was the approaching column. The Army was finally advancing on city. They'd be passing us in a few minutes, and I knew they'd have to stop.

═══ TWELVE ═══

AFTER THE ARMY MOVED THROUGH THEY SET UP A HOS-
pital tent on the outskirts of the city and sent me
there to recuperate. They said I'd be sent home as
soon as I was better, and when they had a few answers. They sent Santiago to Germany because his
wounds were more serious. I heard later that they
made a mess of his neck there, and that he lost his
voice as a result.

In the afternoons the nurses usually agreed to
let me wander off for a while. I often walked down
from the hospital to the beach, where I'd sit and
watch the waves chase up the shore.

Most nights I'd lie awake in the hospital, listening to the distant rattle of gunfire and the explosion of rockets and mortars in the city. The natives
launched mortars at the UN forces and at each
other, while the Army went out on raids trying to
stop them. People on both sides died.

At the hospital I ran into an old friend from the
platoon named Shane. We sat together for hours,

talking about California and Kansas and New York and all the other places we planned to visit back in America. We talked about how there had to be women in those towns who would love us deep down to our soul. But then he left and I was alone again, and those thoughts of love were never enough.

One night a dead shark washed ashore near the hospital. The next morning those of us who could went down to look at it after breakfast. The shark was huge and dark gray, with a white belly. Most of us had never seen anything like it, so we kept our distance. I really wanted to look into the dead shark's eyes, but I never summoned the courage.

One afternoon a nurse from the hospital walked down to the beach with me. We sat on the beach and tried in vain to convince each other to go down and touch the shark.

Soon other soldiers showed up with their cameras and had their pictures taken with it. Then they grew bored with taking pictures and began striking at the shark's mouth with the butts of their M-16s, trying to knock out its teeth. They wanted to make necklaces with them. They eventually stuck their hands in and tried to pry the teeth loose. When I refused to join them, the nurse called down to the others to ask them for one.

In the evening the tide would carry the shark

back out to sea before leaving it on the beach again. After a few days of this the carcass started to smell. Tiny crabs ate its eyes before I could look into them, and before long they were crawling all over its mouth and gills.

Finally a group of engineers brought out a forklift and a flatbed to remove the shark. I watched as the blades of the forklift dug under the shark and lifted it into the air. But when it was just a few feet off the ground its skin burst open and its rotten insides poured to the earth. The stench was something awful.

They called me to the operation tent one morning for a debriefing. They asked me what went wrong. They seemed eager to understand, and they seemed to care. The commander of my division was there, along with a chaplain and a psychologist.

I told them the truth about everything, but somehow I still felt as if I were lying. I told them we'd shot some people and I told them some people had shot at us. And I told them that at this point there was nothing I wanted more than to go home.

They asked about Santiago, and I didn't tell them what he'd said about us never getting right with the world again. I said simply that he was one of ours, and that he'd done his best by the Army and America as far as I saw it.

When they asked me if there was anything else I wanted to tell them, all I could do was repeat that I just wanted to go home. And to say again that I truly hoped Zeller was on some farther shore, and that wherever he was I hoped he would never remember.

In the end, the chaplain put a hand on my shoulder and asked if I was having nightmares. He looked me in the face as the others waited for my response. He said that the doctors and nurses had reported as much, and that he was worried about me. "Do you think this is something that will stay with you?" he asked.

I smiled back weakly, not knowing what to say. But I also knew I had to answer, or they'd send me to someplace awful.

"No," I said. "I'll never remember it all."

As soon as they set up phone lines I called my parents. When I heard my mother's voice I felt as if I'd been hit by a powerful wave. I said hello and she called out to my father.

I asked if she'd seen me on the news, but she said they hadn't even known I was missing until the Army called one night to tell them I'd been found.

"Are you okay?" she asked, the concern evident in her voice.

"I'm fine," I said. Mortars exploded in the distance.

"Everyone's fine here too," she said. "We're all a little worried about you, but otherwise we're just fine. We're praying for you."

"I know," I said.

"Can we send you anything?" she asked.

"I can't really think of anything right now."

Back home fall was upon them. Pennant races and football.

My mother mentioned a few things she could send. Cookies, pumpkin bread, any music I wanted. She said she'd definitely send me a book, perhaps *Don Quixote* this time.

I began to worry that we might be cut off. Some of the operators would cut you off automatically after fifteen minutes on the line. The farther you got from the war the less they enforced this limit, but the division operators were often quick to pull the plug.

"How're the others?" she asked. She knew everyone in my platoon. She'd sent us all cookies once a month when we were at Fort Drum.

"They're fine," I said. This wasn't the time to tell her. I might let her know when I got home, but there were some things mothers shouldn't know. Part of me wanted to tell her right then that I hadn't shot anyone, but again I thought better of it.

"Tell them to make sure they call home," she said.

"I will," I said. Then I warned her that we might

be cut off soon. I told her I loved her and she said she loved me too, and it was all she could do to let me talk to my father.

I could tell by the tone of his voice that my mother was crying. "She hasn't been sleeping," he said. "When do you think you'll be home?"

"Soon." The thought of my mother lying awake and worrying at night was crushing.

"Don't be a hero," my father said. "Just do what you can to get back here."

"I will."

"They never told us you were missing in action," he said.

I thought about Zeller and the others, and how their parents had a few more days of peace because of the delay. There were some things you could never give back.

"They showed them dragging that guy through the streets," my father said. "Did you know him?"

"I met him once," I said. "I knew his name."

"I don't know how," my father said, "but I think your mother saw it too."

I didn't have anything to say to that.

"I try to turn off the news if I can," he said. "Just get yourself back here in one piece."

"I will."

"It'll be okay," he said. "We've always come through all right."

He was right. As a family, our luck had always held.

"I love you," my father said. "Now here's your mom again."

An operator came on the line and said it was time to wrap it up.

"I love you, Mom."

"I love you too," she said. Then there was a click, followed by the silence of thousands of miles.

As I walked back to the hospital I thought about college ahead of me. I wouldn't tell anyone I'd been in the Army. And if they asked why I was a little older, I'd tell them I'd lived abroad, maybe in Prague. I'd tell them the world was a beautiful place. And I'd tell Santiago the same if I ever saw him again.

On the way I decided to walk down to the beach and look out over the ocean. It was around midnight, but the heat was stifling. It was a long way back across the water, but I'd soon be going home, where there were places to hide and places to die. And places to go it alone.

Acknowledgments

I'D LIKE TO THANK ALL THOSE WHO HELPED ME IN ONE way or another through early drafts of this novel, especially Kevin Canty, David James Duncan, Robert Baker, Roger Hedden, Deirdre McNamer, James Crumley, Philip Schneider, Derek Cavens, Robin Troy, and the Million Dollar Workshop. Thank you to everyone at Wichita State and the University of Montana. Thanks to the original composition teacher, Bryan Flores, for teaching me about note cards and plot and sympathy and pilsner at Harry's. And a huge nod goes to Jon Hill, a great friend and voice of reason.

I owe a debt of gratitude to Whitney Terrell, Michelle Boisseau, Wayne Miller, Kevin Prufer, and my colleagues at UCM for making me feel at home.

Those who are and those who were in the military, I hope the best for all of you. Shane Veloni, Vincent Wright, David Banegas, Robert Pettis, Donald Sage, and others from the 10th Mountain, thanks for sharing your stories and memories and hearts in long distance phone calls.

I can't thank everyone at Milkweed enough for making this such a wonderful experience, Patrick, Hilary, and especially Emily. But most of all Daniel Slager for helping me find the heart of the novel and editing it true.

Walter, thank you for giving me the confidence and the courage to live the writing life. And far and above, Cynthia Cannell, thank you for always making me feel like the only one.

Thank you to my family for all their love and support, then and now. Thanks to my mother who had a hard time sleeping while I was there. Thanks to my father who reminds me always that we can defeat the worst part of ourselves and make it out alive and well. And my brother, Josh, I hope you don't mind that I borrowed your name. It turns out I love you that much.

And Katie Cramer Eck, I owe you the deepest praises for seeing something there when you sat next to me for the first time in French class. Thank you for teaching me a new language every step of the way. And of course my Cormac Ulysses. Sing me a song.

Matthew Eck enlisted in the Army in 1992 and served in Somalia and Haiti. He has a BA in English Literature from Wichita State University and received his MFA in Creative Writing from the University of Montana. He currently teaches Creative Writing and Literature at the University of Central Missouri. He lives in Kansas City, Missouri.

The Milkweed National Fiction Prize

Milkweed Editions awards the Milkweed National Fiction Prize to works of high literary quality that embody humane values and contribute to cultural understanding. For more information about the Milkweed National Fiction Prize or to order past winners, visit our Web site (www.milkweed.org) or contact Milkweed Editions at (800) 520-6455.

Driftless
David Rhodes
(2008)

The Farther Shore
Matthew Eck
(2007)

Visigoth
Gary Amdahl
(2006)

Crossing Bully Creek
Margaret Erhart
(2005)

Ordinary Wolves
Seth Kantner
(2004)

Roofwalker
Susan Power
(2002)

Hell's Bottom, Colorado
Laura Pritchett
(2001)

Falling Dark
Tim Tharp
(1999)

Tivolem
Victor Rangel-Ribeiro
(1998)

The Tree of Red Stars
Tessa Bridal
(1997)

The Empress of One
Faith Sullivan
(1996)

Confidence of the Heart
David Schweidel
(1995)

Montana 1948
Larry Watson
(1993)

Larabi's Ox
Tony Ardizzone
(1992)

Aquaboogie
Susan Straight
(1990)

Blue Taxis
Eileen Drew
(1989)

Ganado Red
Susan Lowell
(1988)

Milkweed Editions

FOUNDED IN 1979, MILKWEED EDITIONS IS ONE OF the largest independent, nonprofit literary publishers in the United States. Milkweed publishes with the intention of making a humane impact on society, in the belief that good writing can transform the human heart and spirit.

Join Us

MILKWEED DEPENDS ON THE GENEROSITY OF FOUNDATIONS and individuals like you, in addition to the sales of its books. In an increasingly consolidated and bottom-line-driven publishing world, your support allows us to select and publish books on the basis of their literary quality and the depth of their message. Please visit our Web site (www.milkweed .org) or contact us at (800) 520-6455 to learn more about our donor program.

Special underwriting for this book was contributed by Joanne and Phil Von Blon.

Milkweed Editions, a nonprofit publisher, gratefully acknowledges sustaining support from Anonymous; Emilie and Henry Buchwald; the Bush Foundation; the Patrick and Aimee Butler Family Foundation; the Dougherty Family Foundation; the Ecolab Foundation; the General Mills Foundation; the Claire Giannini Fund; John and Joanne Gordon; William and Jeanne Grandy; the Jerome Foundation; the Lerner Foundation; the McKnight Foundation; Mid-Continent Engineering; a grant from the Minnesota State Arts Board, through an appropriation by the Minnesota State Legislature, a grant from the National Endowment for the Arts, and private funders; Kelly Morrison and John Willoughby; an award from the National Endowment for the Arts, which believes that a great nation deserves great art; the Navarre Corporation; the Starbucks Foundation; the St. Paul Travelers Foundation; Ellen and Sheldon Sturgis; the James R. Thorpe Foundation; the Toro Foundation; Moira and John Turner; United Parcel Service; U. S. Trust Company; Joanne and Phil Von Blon; Kathleen and Bill Wanner; Serene and Christopher Warren; and the W. M. Foundation.

MINNESOTA
STATE ARTS BOARD

NATIONAL
ENDOWMENT
FOR THE ARTS
A great nation
deserves great art.

TARGET®